LAWYER
for the
CAT

LAWYER
for the
CAT

Lee Robinson

THOMAS DUNNE BOOKS
St. Martin's Press
New York

THOMAS DUNNE BOOKS.
An imprint of St. Martin's Press.

LAWYER FOR THE CAT. Copyright © 2016 by Lee Robinson. All rights reserved. Printed in the United States of America. For information, address St. Martin's Press, 175 Fifth Avenue, New York, N.Y. 10010.

www.thomasdunnebooks.com
www.stmartins.com

The Library of Congress Cataloging-in-Publication Data is available upon request.

ISBN 978-1-250-05242-1 (hardcover)
ISBN 978-1-4668-5404-8 (e-book)

Our books may be purchased in bulk for promotional, educational, or business use. Please contact your local bookseller or the Macmillan Corporate and Premium Sales Department at 1-800-221-7945, extension 5442, or by e-mail at MacmillanSpecialMarkets@macmillan.com.

First Edition: May 2016

10 9 8 7 6 5 4 3 2 1

In memory of Virginia Tavel

Acknowledgments

———◆———

I am grateful to Jaime Levine, Anne Brewer, and Jennifer Letwack, my editors, for their insight and enthusiasm.

I am indebted to my agent, Mary Evans, for her vision, wise counsel, and encouragement.

My friend Laura Waggoner Moore read an early draft and provided invaluable advice on pet trusts.

My sister, Salley McInerney, spent a week with me on Edisto as I envisioned this story and introduced me to Gretchen Smith, who graciously led us on a tour of Prospect Hill Plantation.

Thanks also to the Edisto Island Historic Preservation Society, for their good work; and to Cantey Wright and the late Nick Lindsay, whose books on Edisto reflect their deep affection for the place and the people.

My husband, Jerry Winakur, took time away from his own writing to help me with mine. His love keeps me going.

LAWYER
for the
CAT

Let's Start with the Dog

In my twenty-five years as a lawyer I've tried hundreds of cases, represented the full spectrum of humanity: petty thieves from the projects, highborn heroin addicts, the sane and the insane, the abusers and the abused. Every case is a story, and the more preparation I do for a trial, the more complicated that story seems. If I'm not careful I get lost in the labyrinth of facts and law. So the night before a trial I draw a line down the middle of a legal pad. At the top of one column I write "Good," and at the top of the other, "Bad." This is what it's going to boil down to. In last week's divorce case, for example, the list started like this:

Good
Articulate client, will make good witness
Excellent homemaker, mother
Put husband through dental school
Client's husband admits he left because "she got fat"

Bad
Client responsible for large credit card debt
Addicted to Home Shopping Network

Had affair early in marriage with husband's best friend
Drinks too much

And so on. This is what's going to matter. This—after a couple of days of testimony, tears, truths and half-truths and downright lies, lawyers arguing over the rules of evidence, objections overruled and sustained, the judge yawning, the perspiration, the exhaustion—is the story that will matter.

If I were to perform such an analysis on myself, on the Case of My Life, it would look something like this:

Good
Honest
Built successful law practice from scratch
Healthy, not bad-looking
Attentive to aging mother
Generally optimistic
Independent

Bad
Workaholic
Blunt, bordering on obnoxious
Impervious to fashion
Resentful of aging mother
Hot-tempered
A failure at romance

That's what it boils down to: The Good and the Bad of Sarah Bright Baynard, Attorney at Law, AKA Sally, just turned fifty.

. . .

"I hate the sound of it," I say.

"What are you talking about?" asks my best friend, Ellen. We're at Giminiano's, the new restaurant on King Street that's tucked behind a shoe store, down a narrow brick walkway. It's advertised as "lively and intimate," which means—as we now understand—tiny, noisy, and crowded.

"Fifty. It sounds so heavy, like some giant sack of years I'll be lugging around for the rest of my life."

"That doesn't sound like you," she says.

"Maybe now that I'm fifty I'm not the same *me* anymore."

"Wow," Ellen says. "You definitely need a glass of wine, or two or three. Red or white?"

"Shouldn't we wait for the others?" Every year Ellen assembles the same group of girlfriends to celebrate my birthday. We were all roommates in law school, but she's the only one I've stayed close to. Ellen thinks she's doing me a favor by getting us together, as if this annual reunion will magically transport me back to my twenties, but it depresses me. This year I postponed it a couple of times with lame excuses, until I couldn't put it off any longer.

"Answer the question. Red or white?" Her voice has that prosecutorial determination she uses in the courtroom.

"Red, I guess."

She scans the wine list, motions for the waiter. "We'd like a bottle of Chianti. The Banfi, please." Ellen is one of those people who knows her wines. She's also a great tennis player and gardener, not to mention lawyer, wife, and mother. I'd hate her except for the fact that she's one of the very few people who knows me well and loves me anyway.

By the time the wine comes Valerie and Wendy have arrived. Valerie looks great, her thick red hair swept up and pinned loosely in one of those arrangements that looks artsy and casual but undoubtedly takes a lot of time. "Helen sends her regrets," she says. "Last-minute babysitting for the grandchildren."

"God," says Wendy, "Can you believe we're old enough to have grandchildren?" There's a moment of discomfort, a pang of silence in which I wonder if they're all thinking the same thing: *Yes, we're all old enough, but one of us won't ever have grandchildren.*

Ellen, bless her heart, recovers quickly, lifts her glass toward me: "To Sally, who gets better every year!" I lift mine, take a swallow big enough, I hope, to bring me back to myself, whoever that is.

"Yeah," says Wendy, "I heard things are getting better for you in the love department!" She leans across the table and lowers her voice. It's only then that I notice the little pucker-lines around her mouth; otherwise she could pass for thirty-five. "He's a vet, right?"

"Just a good friend at this point," I say.

"She's being coy, if it's possible for Sally to be coy!" Ellen says. She pours the rest of the bottle into my glass, orders another. "Maybe, since he's a vet," she says, "he could help you with the cat case."

"*Katz?*" Valerie says, her eyes widening. "Don't tell me the Katzes are divorcing!"

"'Cat,' as in feline," I say. "But it's not official yet."

"She did such a good job on the dog case, the probate judge wants her to represent a cat," explains Ellen, as if I'm not there. And then, because the chatter around us makes it hard to hear, she continues in her loud, lawyer-in-the-courtroom voice: "You know about her thing with the dog, right?" Of course it is at this very moment that the waiter reappears, and although he can't miss hearing "her thing with the dog" he pretends, as he takes our orders, that he hasn't. We smother our laughter until he leaves, then explode. Everyone in the room turns around to look.

"Okay," says Valerie, after we've recovered our respectability, "I want the whole story."

"Sorry," I say. "Client confidentiality."

"Bullshit," says Ellen. "Your client was a dog. A dog doesn't have any secrets."

"So, tell all," insists Valerie.

When I'm finished she says, "So, let me get this straight: Joe Baynard, judge of the Charleston Family Court, who happens to be your ex-husband, appoints you to represent a schnauzer in a divorce case, not because the dog really needs a lawyer but because he—Joe—is still in love with you?"

"Well, to be fair to him," I said, "it was the case from hell, and poor Sherman—"

"Sherman?"

"The dog. Sherman was right in the middle of it. Like a kid in the middle of a custody case."

"So," says Wendy, "Joe couldn't find someone else? He has to choose his ex-wife to represent the dog?"

"He's appointed me in lots of custody cases—to represent the kids," I say. "I think he was hoping I'd help him settle it."

"Maybe," says Ellen, "but he's also obsessed with you."

"Joe's remarried, isn't he?" asks Valerie.

"I heard they were separated," says Wendy.

"They separated for a while, but they're back together now," I say.

"I always liked Joe," says Wendy. "I never did really understand why you . . . Never mind, this is your birthday dinner!"

"So, what happened . . . with"—Valerie interrupts herself while the waiter serves our appetizers—"with the case, I mean?"

"The couple reconciled and Sherman's back home with them."

"She's leaving out the best part," says Ellen. "The dog's vet wants to marry her."

Valerie's eyebrows rise. "You're getting *married*?"

"Not anytime soon," I say.

"I don't know what you're waiting for," says Ellen. "He's perfect for you."

And there's a voice in my head—a voice that sounds strangely like my own. This voice, this me, is agreeing with Ellen. This me is still Sally Baynard, lawyer extraordinaire, but she's also a woman with a love life, one who doesn't live with her demented mother. She trusts her own instincts, isn't afraid of making another mistake.

This me might have another glass of wine, might even move in with the vet.

By the time I get back to the condo, after dinner and dessert and coffee, I'm my old self again, feeling the full load of being Sarah Bright Baynard for half a century. The short drive across town was oddly comforting—Charleston with its antebellum buildings glowing under streetlamps, cobblestone streets with their bumpy history, the city where I'm still, by contrast, young—but when I enter the renovated lobby of my building (faux marble floor, trendy red leather furniture) I'm struck by its gleaming newness. The members of the home owners' board are all in their seventies and eighties. Maybe this expensive facelift is a defense against their own deterioration. This year there are fresh Christmas decorations—real pine garlands with white bows over the doors, a gigantic spruce tree in one corner, glittering with tiny white lights—to replace the fake wreaths and faded red ribbons of years past.

I share the elevator with a woman who lives on my floor, whose name I don't remember, and her poodle, whose name I *do* remember. "Hello, Curly," I say, and the dog wags her tail.

"I hope you'll bring your mother to the holiday party," says the woman. "She could meet some of our neighbors! There's a very nice older man who's just moved into the penthouse."

"I'm sure it will be a lovely event." I remember last year's party. I showed up in slacks and a sweater, my mother in a black wool dress and pearls. Most of the other women were in sequins and chiffons. Mom took one look and insisted on going back up to our apartment to change clothes. By the time we got back, the crab dip and the ham biscuits had been devoured.

"Where's your little friend—that adorable schnauzer?" asks the woman.

"Sherman's gone back to his family. I was just taking care of him for a few days."

"Oh, that's a shame. It must have been hard to let him go!"

"Yes." Now I remember: It's Mrs. Furley, rhymes with Curly. Josephine Furley. She has a head of black ringlets, dyed to match her dog's.

"Well, then, you must get one of your own!" she says as we walk down the hall. "Your mother would like that, wouldn't she? And then when she's gone—I know you don't want to think about that, dear . . . but when she's gone, you won't be all alone."

Of course I won't tell Mrs. Furley the truth: that it's actually not at all hard for me to think about life without my mother. Maybe I'm a terrible person, but I often imagine this apartment to myself, these rooms that feel so cramped with her furniture, the equipment left over from the last hospitalization (the walker, the bedside potty), not to mention the bottles of pills and the giant-sized bottles of Metamucil that crowd the kitchen counter. It's not scary at all to imagine coming home to silence, to my own space, without Mom and her sitters: Delores on weekdays and Shenille on nights and weekends if I need her. I would miss Delores, with her great laugh and good sense, but sometimes I sit out on my little balcony overlooking the harbor and imagine how it will be when I'm free of them all.

"You don't have to do this," my friend Ellen said, the last time I complained. "Your mother wouldn't want this for you."

"I can't put her in a nursing home. I thought I could, but—"

"You deserve a life."

"I have a life."

"You know what I mean," she said. "Like maybe a life with Tony." Tony is the vet. "I'm beginning to think you're using your mother as an excuse not to make a commitment."

"Mom has nothing to do with it. We're just taking our time."

"Bullshit. He's crazy about you. And you know what I think about you and your damn 'time'? I think you're running out of it."

Maybe Ellen's right, and undoubtedly Shenille, who's sitting in the living room watching a sappy romantic movie, would agree. She looks up at me, scans my outfit (white silk blouse, black pants, silver earrings), opines, "You're still kind of pretty for your age. Seems like there'd be some nice man out there for you." Shenille is overly generous with such observations, but she's also very patient with my mother (who once referred to her as "the sweet little white one," to distinguish her from Delores) so I ignore the comment.

She gives me a brief report on Mom's evening—she ate all her dinner except the broccoli, spilled some juice on her bathrobe (in the dryer now), went to sleep after *America's Got Talent*—and hands me a piece of paper on which she's written a name and a number. "He called right after you left. Said something about a cat case. I told him I didn't expect you back till late, but he kept on talking, about how his mama was crazy. Sounded kinda crazy himself, but I guess you're used to crazy people, with all those divorces you do." She says 'divorces' as if it's a nasty word. She's twenty, recently married, and has told me (another unsolicited observation) that she would never, ever get a divorce, because "no judge can divide what God has bound together." She gathers her purse, her jacket. "Oh, and he said he's a friend of your husband. That's what made me think maybe he had the wrong—"

"He probably meant my ex."

"He was talking so fast I got confused." She gathers her purse, her sweater. "See you tomorrow night, Ms. Baynard."

"I wish you'd call me Sally."

"But your checks, they say Sarah."

"Sally's my nickname."

"Sarah's prettier. Like, more fancy or something."

I check on my mother, who's sleeping soundly, then settle into bed myself, read until the book falls on my chest, turn off the light, then can't go back to sleep. I miss the vet. I miss the smell of him.

We could have this all the time, he said last weekend. We were lying in the hammock on his screened porch overlooking the creek, under a blanket because it was chilly. The three dogs—Susie and Sheba, his two golden retrievers, and Carmen, the beagle abandoned by her owner—stayed close, Carmen's tail thwacking the floor contentedly, in rhythm with the hammock.

I have my practice, I said. *And my mother. This place is too small for the three of us. And what about when your son visits?*

Then we'll get a bigger place.

And I'll commute every day?

Or I will. I told you I'd be willing to do that.

That doesn't make any sense. Your clinic's right down the road. It's a perfect setup for you.

He rolled halfway out of the hammock, stuck his foot out to make it stop swinging. *If you don't want it to work, Sally, you can find a hundred reasons why it won't.*

I'm just trying to point out—

Spare me the lawyerly logic!

I followed him into the kitchen. The dogs followed, too. *I just want us to take our time*, I said. *I don't want to screw it up.*

That's what you say about Carmen. He poured himself some juice, didn't offer me any. *Here's this wonderful animal*—he reached down, scratched the beagle under the chin—*who needs somebody to love her. You say you want her, but somehow you can never bring yourself to take her home. Do I see a pattern here?*

Okay, I said. *I'll do it.*

Which, take the dog, or marry me?

Let's start with the dog, I said.

He laughed. Thank God he laughed. *One thing at a time, I guess*, he said. *You want to take her tonight?*

Not tonight. Soon. I promise.

He pulled me close. *Just don't break this poor animal's heart, okay?*

Trouble All Over It

———◆———

Most of the Probate Court is housed on the fourth floor of the new judicial center, but Judge Clarkson's office is in the old courthouse on the corner of Meeting and Broad—"The Historic Courthouse," they call it—and this seems appropriate for a judge about to retire, who's spent most of his life dealing with the business of the deceased: wills and trusts, testators and executors, the detritus of the dead.

Probate Court is foreign territory for me. I know my way around the Circuit Court and Family Court. In my younger days as a public defender I handled hundreds of criminal cases in the Circuit Court, defending the indefensible. And these days I spend almost all my time in the Family Court. I know its courtrooms and corridors as well as I know my own condo. The clerks and deputies call me Sally. The judges all know me, too. One of them, the Honorable Joseph H. Baynard, is my ex-husband. Once, when a client protested, "You can't possibly understand what it's like to go through this!" I could say, in all honesty, *Yes, I do.* And I knew better than to send her off, after I'd handed her a certified copy of the divorce decree, with a silly

"Congratulations!" because I've learned the hard way that this piece of paper might end the marriage, but it doesn't end the sadness.

This morning in the Probate Court I feel like a neophyte lawyer all over again. I don't even know which way to turn when I get off the elevator. It's reassuring, then, when the woman behind the sliding glass window says, "Ms. Baynard, Judge Clarkson's expecting you. He's in his chambers. First door on the left."

The judge rises slowly from behind his desk, which is almost completely covered by stacks of files. "Old cases," he says, "going to storage. Time to retire them, like me." We shake hands. "Baynard," he says, as if he's taste-testing the name. He has a bulbous nose, outsized ears, a shiny bald head. "You married John Baynard's son. From upstate, aren't you?"

"Yes, sir. Columbia." No need to go into the divorce if he doesn't remember.

"This cat case . . . Have a seat. . . . Thought I'd seen it all until this one. Heard you like animals."

"I like them, sir, but I'm not sure that qualifies me—"

"Oh, don't sell yourself short."

"I don't do probate work, Your Honor."

"I know that. You stay over there in the Family Court most of the time, don't you?" He breathes heavily, as if talking is too much exertion.

"These days, yes sir."

"Well, that's perfect. Then you know how to handle yourself in a cat fight!" He laughs hard, pats his plentiful belly as if to congratulate himself on being so clever. "Seriously, I hear you don't let anyone push you around."

"Not if I can help it."

"Heard about that dog case. You managed that one pretty well, I'm told."

"It sort of settled itself."

"Anyway, this cat case . . . very unusual. Ever heard of a pet trust?"

"Like Leona Helmsley?"

"Exactly. She set one up for her dog. . . . What was its name?"

"Trouble."

"Right. Anyway," the judge continues, "I've seen a few of these trusts since the law was passed here in South Carolina. They're usually pretty straightforward, but this one's got trouble written all over it!" Again he laughs, pats his belly. "But mind you, I'm not asking you to do this pro bono. There's plenty of money in it for the trust enforcer."

"The what?"

His chair squeaks as he swivels around to the bookcase behind him, pulls a volume out, opens the book to a page he's marked. "Here. Section 62-7-408: *Trust for care of animal.* 'A trust authorized by this section may be enforced by a person appointed in the terms of the trust or, if no person is so appointed, by a person appointed by the court.' That's where you come in. The settlor—that's the deceased, Lila Mackay—didn't appoint an enforcer, so I'm going to do that." He slams the book shut. "You want my set of the Code? Can't even give it away."

"No, sir, but thank you."

"I know, all you young'uns do your research on the computer, right?"

"I can't really call myself a 'young'un' anymore, but yes, I do my research on the computer."

"Not the same, though," he says, "as with the books."

"It's faster."

"Maybe, but you don't feel the heft."

"Sir?"

"These books, they've got the weight of history in them. Sometimes you need to feel it. Anyway, as I was saying, since Mrs. Mackay didn't appoint a trust enforcer, I'm going to do that, considering the amount of money involved and the, uh, rather elaborate terms of the trust. Here, I've made a copy for you. Read on down to paragraph 5, and you'll see what our problem is. Burney should have advised her against that, if you ask me."

"Burney?"

"Her lawyer. Burney Haynes. Had his office out there on Edisto Island, near Lila. Honest fellow, but had no business handling an estate of this size. Never did understand the first rule of practicing law: *Don't mess around with what you don't know.* Dead now, so he can't do any more harm. Take a look at paragraph 5 and you'll see what I mean."

I read out loud: " 'I hereby appoint one of the following as caregiver for my cat, Beatrice, to be chosen by the Probate Judge at the time of my death or at such time as I may become unable to care for Beatrice myself: Gail Sims, my groundskeeper; Katherine Harleston, Assistant Librarian, Charleston County Library; Dr. Philip Freeman, my nephew; or any other suitable person.' "

"Now," he says, "does anything strike you as strange about all this?"

"This phrase 'or any other suitable person.' It's almost like she wanted to make it complicated," I say.

The judge nods. "Like I said, it's unusual. Keep reading."

" 'I direct that the chosen caregiver shall reside with Beatrice, during Beatrice's lifetime, at my home, Oak Bluff Plantation, on Edisto Island, South Carolina, and shall endeavor to provide Beatrice with the same lifestyle, routine, and emotional environment as she has become accustomed to in my care.' "

"You see what I mean," says the judge. "What the hell is a cat's 'emotional environment'? You can bet old Burney didn't come up with that poppycock—it's got Lila written all over it—but he should have advised her against it."

"I guess 'emotional environment' means she wanted the caregiver to love the cat as much as she did."

"Look at Paragraph 8. . . . You think fifty thousand dollars a year is enough for loving a cat?"

"Wow. And what's this about some notebooks?"

"She left a box of stuff—I didn't go through it, but it looks like she kept notes on the cat—and those go to the caregiver." He points to two cardboard boxes on the floor. "I'll have it all delivered to your office."

"It's an interesting case, but I don't know what you need *me* for. There's a trustee, right?"

"South State Bank, but their role is solely to manage the money. I need someone to choose the caretaker and make sure the cat's properly cared for."

"But this says . . . *you're* to choose the caregiver."

"Like I told you, old Burney should have advised her against that. I'm retiring."

"I hadn't heard that."

"January first."

"But couldn't you—"

"I'm old, I'm tired, and my wife is ill. The new associate judge, Ann Wilson . . . I don't want to burden her with something like this when she's just starting out. You know Ann?"

"Not personally. She's a good bit younger than I am."

"You women are taking over," he says. "Anyway, you'll need to interview the people Lila named, then make a decision. Like I said, the statute gives me the authority to appoint a trust enforcer—that will be you—and the trust assets are quite sufficient to pay your fee."

"What are the assets?"

"Three million, plus the plantation on Edisto—three hundred acres and the house."

"Where did all that money come from?"

"Her husband, Verner Mackay, died a while back. A moneymaking machine if there ever was one. Kept up with the stock market minute by minute. Lila was the opposite. Never did care much about money, but when she met him she was about to lose her family place—Oak Bluff—and he was rich enough to keep it up."

"You knew her well?"

"Distant cousin. She was always irrational about that old place. Should have sold it a long time ago."

"What happens when the cat dies?"

"The money goes to the ASPCA, the plantation property goes to her son Randall. Which reminds me—steer clear of him."

"He's been calling me," I say, "but I thought I ought to talk to you first, before I call him back."

"He's mad as hell because he won't get his hands on the real estate until the cat dies."

"I guess I can't blame him."

"But Lila was plenty generous to him when he was young, set him up in a string of businesses. All of them failed. He's a spoiled brat, with a bad temper."

"He's dangerous?"

"Oh, I think he's mostly talk, but he came up here the other day on a rampage, demanded to see me, went on and on about how his mother was incompetent when she arranged the trust. *You go right ahead,* I told him. *You go hire yourself a hotshot lawyer if you want to,* but I warned him that if he tries to set the trust aside on the grounds of lack of capacity, and he fails, he stands to lose the remainder—what he's entitled to after the cat dies. Burney Haynes wasn't the sharpest tack in the box but at least he remembered to include the standard penalty clause for contesting."

Now I'm feeling like the neophyte lawyer again. "I don't understand."

"If he contests the validity of the trust and loses, and the court finds that there's no probable cause for his challenge, he forfeits what she left for him. Lila was eccentric, but that's not enough to set a trust aside."

"How did he . . . the son . . . how did he even know I was involved?"

"Because I took the liberty of informing him that I'm appointing you as trust enforcer," he says.

"But, sir, I haven't even agreed—"

"Like I said, I'd steer clear of him. Randall's always had a screw loose. Now, you better get to work. . . . Lila, bless her soul, would have approved of you. She was always a women's libber." He stands, shakes my hand. "You'll want to get going on this right away," he says.

"There's a rush?"

"Well, I guess there really isn't, as long as you don't mind keeping the cat for a while. She's out there with my secretary. You can take her now, or I'll have her delivered to your office this afternoon."

"I can't take the cat!"

He smiles. "I've done my homework on you. You're tough as nails. You were damn good in criminal court and you're downright *ferocious* in divorce court, so don't tell me you can't handle a little old cat!"

The two blocks back to my office are torture: How can a cat be so heavy? I hold the carrier by its metal handle until my fingers go numb, then pull it up to my chest and wrap my arms around it. The cat lurches backward, yowls. She's all black, except for the eyes: huge, yellow, afraid.

He Doesn't Get a Veto

———◆———

Natalie Carter, my afternoon client, is waiting in the reception area when I walk in with the cat, who starts up again with her yowling. I can't wait to put the carrier down—my back is killing me—and I drop it maybe a little too hard onto the floor.

"Jeez," says Gina, my secretary. "She's really upset." She stoops down, peers inside. "Calm down, honey. We're not going to hurt you."

"I'm allergic to cats," says Mrs. Carter. Natalie's allergic to everything: peanuts, dairy products, her husband.

"I'll watch her. I'm good with animals," Gina says. "See, she's already settling down, just being here. Isn't that right, gorgeous? I knew you'd be fine once you got used to us." It's obvious the cat's appearance is no surprise to Gina. I give her a look that says, *We'll talk about this later.*

Natalie follows me back to my office. "So," Natalie says as she settles herself on the sofa, crossing her legs and smoothing her skirt, "Derwood's being a real bastard, isn't he?"

"I knew he wouldn't be easy to deal with." In the days I was a public defender I had the misfortune of appearing before Derwood Carter, a Circuit Court judge from Beaufort, when he was presiding in Charleston. He's a sanctimonious snob who doles out maximum sentences for minor offenses, giving speeches about moral rectitude. Meanwhile it's common knowledge that he's been bonking his court reporter for years. Now, in his own divorce case, he's insisting on representing himself.

"But he's worse than you imagined, right?" Natalie says.

"It would make things a lot easier if he'd just hire an attorney, but I can't force him to do that."

"He thinks he's smarter than everybody else," she says. "Including every lawyer in South Carolina, and including me, of course. He thinks I'm dumb as a rock, and maybe I am, putting up with him for twenty-five years. You know why I married him? Not because he was a lawyer, although I admit that didn't hurt. Not because he comes from a fancy family." She reaches in her purse for a pack of cigarettes, takes one out, then sees my expression. "Don't worry, I know I can't smoke in here. . . . Anyway, I married him because he told me I had the most beautiful body he'd ever seen. Can you imagine?"

No, I can't. I know Tony likes my body, but even if it were perfect, which it certainly isn't, he would never say anything like that.

"And this offer he's made," she continues, "just goes to show how dumb he thinks I am. Twenty percent of our assets, and no alimony. It's insulting."

"Let's talk about a response, and if we can't make some progress toward a reasonable settlement in the next couple of weeks, we'll just have to battle it out."

"I don't think I can take it . . . a trial, I mean." She clings to the cigarette as if it's her only friend.

"You have a strong case. From the fault standpoint, we have the detective's report, which clearly establishes that every time he travels out of town to hold court, he spends the night with his court reporter. And you—"

"But he says he's earned all our money, and all I've done is spend, spend, spend."

"You've got a solid record of homemaker contributions, Natalie, and you were his secretary while he got his law practice going, right?"

"But when I talk to him——"

"Stop talking to him." I told her that last time we met.

"I know, my therapist says that too. But he comes by the house to check on things—'my property,' he calls it, as if I don't have any right to live there—and then he wants to talk about the boys. He says this divorce is breaking their hearts. That they'll hate me for it." Now she's crying. I hand her the box of tissues. She blows her nose. "You must think I'm just a big stupid baby!"

"I know it's hard, Natalie, but you'll get through it. Why don't you take a break, have a cigarette? And while you're outside, think about what you're going to do with your life after the divorce. When you come back, I want you to tell me what you see yourself doing in five years."

"Derwood says——"

"No, not what Derwood says. What *Natalie* says, what *Natalie* thinks, what *Natalie* wants. I want you to have a vision for yourself. Okay?"

When she leaves I pick up the phone, call the vet's office. His receptionist recognizes my voice, says he's busy with an emergency. "Maureen, I need to bring a cat in this afternoon."

"She's been here before?"

"I'm just taking care of her temporarily."

"Then we'll have to get the owner's consent," she says.

"I'm her temporary guardian. I have a court order."

"Ma'am?"

"I'll explain it when I get there. This cat seems kind of ornery, or upset or something. Maybe she's sick. I don't know anything about cats, so—"

"Bring her out around five thirty, then."

When Natalie Carter comes back she seems more relaxed. "So," I start, "let's talk about five years from now."

She takes a deep breath. "You'll think I'm dreaming."

"I'm listening."

"I want to take over my dad's landscaping business. It's that little place out on Highway 21, you might have seen it. He's ready to retire, and he's talked about selling it, but I've always liked working with plants. I've done some small projects for friends. If I could partner with a landscape architect we could do . . . There's a big demand now for designs using native plants."

"That's a great idea."

"For example," she says, going over to the window, "that garden there, behind the stucco house . . . it needs some help. I'm not talking about a manicured, formal look, but something graceful, casual, with plantings that don't need a lot of attention." Her hands move as if she's designing in the air. "But I'll need some money. I can't expect Dad to give me the business."

"You'll come out of this with money, Natalie. I just can't predict how much until we're a little further along."

"So you don't think I'm crazy? I mentioned it to Derwood once and he said—"

"Derwood doesn't get a veto."

She smiles. It's the first time I've seen her smile like this. "I like that," she says. " 'Derwood doesn't get a veto.' "

"So let's talk about our counteroffer."

. . .

When Natalie leaves I buzz Gina. "We need to have a talk about the cat."

"It's not *my* fault," she says.

"You won't be convicted without a fair trial."

"She's kind of settling down, so if you're going to yell—"

I'm not going to yell. I'd like to, but I won't. I know how this is going to go: I'll tell Gina, very calmly, that I understand she's friends with Maria Lopez, clerk of Probate Court, and I know they talk all the time. That's how Maria heard about the dog case. That's why Judge Clarkson thought of me for the cat case. Fine, so far; I guess I'm flattered. But there's a difference between a cat *case* and a cat. I didn't know I'd end up with a cat. But Gina knew. Of course she did.

Gina will say something like, *But it's not really such a big deal, is it? To keep her for a little while?* And then she'll remind me that pets aren't allowed in her apartment building, otherwise she'd take Beatrice herself.

And I'll say, *It's the principle of the thing. It was my decision to make, and I didn't have all the facts.* And then, despite my determination to stay calm, I'll snap: *I'd appreciate it if you'd at least let me cling to the illusion that I'm the boss here.*

When we're finished she'll apologize and I'll thank her for the apology, but we'll both know that this conversation, this feeble assertion of my authority, won't change a thing. Like old married people who drive each other crazy, whose arguments are predictable, we follow our well-rehearsed script, we yell and cry and pout and in the end we always make up.

And it isn't because we're a natural pair. When Gina turns fifty in a couple of months, she'll greet it as merely one more mile marker on the grand adventure of her life. She goes to the gym three times a week, running as fast as she can from old age. She's stopped asking me to come with her. I can't stand being around all those women in their skintight shiny outfits, panting and sweating. I look at myself in the mirror—those awful huge mirrors—in my T-shirt and shorts and dingy sneakers and think, *God, who is that woman?*

Gina's beauty is almost a handicap. She's been divorced twice, both times from men who couldn't tolerate the attention she gets just walking down the street. Now she's dating Rick Silber, my former client, and of course she's absolutely *certain* he's the one. Her optimism endures despite her history. Maybe she's right, though she and Rick make a strange couple: the perpetually positive former beauty queen and the neurotic psychology professor who used to come to my office in Bermuda shorts, sandals, and socks.

When we shook hands outside the courthouse, after I'd handed him a certified copy of his divorce decree, he thanked me and asked my permission to take Gina out.

"She's a free woman, Rick."

"I know that, but I thought I'd run it past you. I value your advice."

"Well, if you're asking for my advice about Gina, I'll be honest. She doesn't need another man who worships her pretty face. She needs a partner who—"

"Who respects her?"

"Exactly. She's smart as hell. I couldn't run my practice without her."

He laughed, a rare thing for Rick Silber: "That's what she tells me!"

Zooming Out

—◈—

I'd envisioned a drive out to the country, to Tony's clinic on John's Island, with Beatrice in her carrier on the backseat of my Camry, and dinner afterward with him (the cat having been examined and treated for whatever condition was making her so ornery, then safely boarded in his kennel), and after dinner maybe an hour or two at his house on the creek before I drove back to town to let the sitter go for the night.

But Delores couldn't stay late and when I called Shenille to ask her if she could come in for a couple of hours, she sounded terrible. "It's just a cold," she said. "I can do it if you really need me."

"No, of course not. I'll take Mom with me."

"You sure?"

"Yes, we'll be fine. Take care of yourself."

But now I'm stalled in traffic on Highway 17 with my mother in the backseat complaining that she has to pee and Beatrice in her carrier on the seat beside her, complaining about whatever cats complain about. "Okay," I said when we were starting out and Mom insisted on riding with the cat, "she can sit next to you, but you'll have to promise me"—I took both her hands and held them firmly in the way I do when I'm trying to get her full attention—"you won't let her out of her carrier."

"I have to *go!*" she says now.

"Can you hold it for fifteen minutes?" In the rearview mirror I see her nod, but I'm not reassured. She has frequent accidents, wears pads in her underpants during the day. And the "fifteen minutes" is a fiction. We're hardly moving. Beatrice yowls accusingly, as if she knows where I'm taking her. I turn the radio to the classical station— maybe music will calm her—but it's some contemporary cacophony, a theme song for our distress.

Half an hour later I reach across for my purse (I'll call Tony, thank him for waiting), but when my hand finds a soft hump, it isn't the purse. It's Beatrice, in the passenger seat. She looks at me with an expression of mild disdain, her head held high, as if to say, *If you don't mind, I prefer the front.* When I brake suddenly she stiffens, claws the seat to steady herself.

"Sorry," I say, and she relaxes. "I'm taking you to a place where they'll be really nice to you. You'll like it there, I promise." She looks at me again with those yellow eyes, unblinking, a creature not easily fooled. She reminds me of my aunt Emma, my mother's older sister, dead ten years now. "No wonder she never married," Mom used to say. "She's always glaring at you like she thinks you're stupid. And she's so tactless!"

When I visited Aunt Emma in the hospital near the end, I brought her some flowers. "You should have saved these for the funeral," she said.

"Oh, Aunt Emma, you're not dying!" She looked at me, her eyes as clear and determined as I'd ever seen them, and said: "I'm not a fool, you know."

Aunt Emma always had cats, two or three at a time. "The thing about cats," she told me once, "is that they know what they need from us, and it isn't much. They need to be fed and petted, but they don't need their humans fawning over them all the time. They want loyalty and respect. Remember that, and you'll get along fine."

Tony has the cat on his exam table. "Nice to see you, Margaret," he says with a nod to my mother, who's feeling better after using the restroom. "Okay, sweetheart," he says as he runs his fingers down the cat's spine, "will you let me feel your belly? How old is she?"

"I don't really don't know much about her." I give him a short summary of the cat case. "There's a box of stuff back at the office, maybe . . . ."

He checks the tag hanging from her collar. "Rabies vaccine is current, but you'll have to renew it in March."

"No way I'll have her *that* long!"

"She doesn't have a temperature. I could run some tests, but she seems fine, really. Just a little overweight, aren't you, honey?"

"I am not!" says my mother.

"He's not talking about you, Mom."

"No, ma'am, you look lovely, as always," he says. "What are you feeding her?" he asks me.

"I just got her today. I wasn't expecting—"

"I'll give you some samples until you can go shopping. Since you don't know what she's accustomed to, get some high-quality dry stuff, and some canned. Try the dry first—it's better for weight loss— but if she won't eat that, mix in some of the canned. Cats can be finicky."

None of this is reassuring me. "You won't board her for a while?"

"We don't generally do long-term boarding."

"It should only be a week or two, while I do my investigation."

He laughs. "You hear that, Beatrice? This woman wants to abandon you already!" He hands the cat to me. "Hold her between her front legs, like this, so she feels secure." He takes his white coat off, tosses it in the hamper. "So, would you ladies like to join me for dinner? What do you say, Margaret?" My mother beams.

"What about the cat?" I ask.

"The cat will be fine at my place as long as we keep her in the carrier. I'll pick up some seafood and meet you there. Fried oysters okay?"

"This is where Tony lives," I tell Mom. We've taken the dirt road that winds through the marsh.

"Tony?"

"The vet. You can't see it now, but the creek's back there, behind the house."

"He could use a better yard man," she says. When she talks like this she's so much like her old self, it's hard for me to believe she has Alzheimer's. Never once in her life did she have a regular "yard man," but that doesn't matter—she considers herself the kind of woman who *ought* to have one.

I know the house will disappoint her. It's comfortable enough, but small: a kitchen/den combination, two bedrooms, a tiny bathroom. Its saving grace is the big screened porch in the back, facing the creek, furnished with a hammock, an old sofa, and a picnic table.

Tony hardly ever locks the doors. The dogs, he says, are his security system. "They won't bite, but they make a helluva lot of noise." His two golden retrievers, Susie and Sheba, bound out of the darkness of the hallway, barking. Behind them comes Carmen the beagle, baying with her nose in the air. "Hush, girls, it's just me." Mom grips my arm, pulls back. The cat lurches in the carrier. I turn on the light—a cascade of dust from the lamp shade, a stack of unopened mail on the hall table. "They won't bite, Mom."

I lift the carrier to the kitchen counter, safe from the dogs' curious noses. "Sit here. We'll eat at this table."

"But there's nothing to eat."

"Tony's bringing something from a restaurant."

"He lives here by himself?"

"The dogs keep him company. And his son visits." Jake lives in California with his mother. "He's thirteen." I pour her a glass of water.

"Terrible age," she says, pointing at me, wagging her finger: "You were so . . . awful!"

Breathe, I tell myself, and open the cabinet where he keeps the plates. I can't find three that match. "That was a hard time for both of us, Mom. We'd just lost Dad."

She takes a sip of water, holding the glass lightly as if it's the finest crystal, her little finger extended. "Will Dad be home for dinner?" she asks. Delores, her favorite sitter, would know how to handle this. *Let her live in her own world,* she says. *Easier on her, easier on you.*

"No, Mom, not tonight." Before she can ask another question Tony comes with the food: fried oysters, hush puppies, slaw. The dogs dance around him until he fills their bowls. The cat has pressed herself against the back of the carrier, about as far away from them as she can get.

"I brought some cat food samples," Tony says, "and a bag of litter. You'll need to get more of both. I also brought a litter box from the clinic, until you have time to shop for one. But maybe you should wait until you get home to feed her. The dogs are probably a bit much for her."

I imagine how the scene would look to a stranger: a man, a woman, husband and wife, at their kitchen table. Her mother (of course there's a clear resemblance) eating slowly, cutting each oyster in half, leaving the hush puppies on the plate. The man and his wife trading stories of the workday, this dinnertime much like the others in their history of dinnertimes. The dogs finish their food, settle in the living room.

Zoom out, and the little house almost glows with satisfaction. They're in this together.

This is the way he wants me to see it. But I'm always zooming out too far, into the future, where they argue, where the wife resents the long commute or the husband hates living in town, where the old woman drives him crazy but he's too nice to admit it, and the wife— she must be crazy, too, because she can't bring herself to put her mother in a nursing home. And out there, not very far, there's a boy. He won't visit often, and maybe he's as sweet as his father, but what thirteen-year-old (see, the old woman's pointing her finger) isn't sometimes really awful?

And then there's the cat. An orphan cat who needs a good home.

The Mess We Make of It

I'm organizing the stuff in the cat box," says Gina. She's in the conference room, sorting papers into piles. "I'll have it finished by the time of the deposition."

"What? There can't be a deposition yet."

"Not in the cat case. The Vernelle divorce. We rescheduled for Friday morning, remember? I'll have the table cleared off by then. . . . What's the matter? You look like hell." Other lawyers have secretaries who flatter them. I have Gina.

"I had a terrible night."

"Please don't tell me you've screwed up the vet thing."

"As a matter of fact," I say, "we had a perfectly *delightful* dinner at his place. He invited my mother, too. I think he actually likes her."

"Then he's a saint. And so sexy. You're crazy to keep putting him off." She pulls some papers out of the box. "Can you believe this stuff? I thought it was all supposed to be about the cat, but there are a bunch of letters here, and some kind of weird diary or something."

"Anything about what she eats?"

"Nothing that practical. So, what was so terrible—about last night, I mean?"

I'm sleep-deprived, but I do my best to describe our visit to the twenty-four-hour PetSmart on the way back from Tony's. We entered the enormous store, me lugging the carrier, my mother leaning on my other arm until I got a cart and reminded her that she could use it as a walker. "You're doing fine," she said to Beatrice, who didn't seem to mind riding in it.

I searched for a litter box (a dizzying array: boxes that mechanically sift the litter, covered ones that trap the smell) and food (again a veritable cornucopia: plain and "gourmet," and "organic"). I settled on a plain plastic box, the cheapest litter, and the same brands of food Tony had given me samples of. Then I changed my mind and went back, adding some organic canned stuff because the picture looked so much more appetizing and switching the plain litter box for a fancier one. My mother, meanwhile, was fascinated by the rack of "Feline Fashions": hoodies, coats (leopard print!), even a pink tutu. I had to tear her away, but then she glided right past the checkout with the cart, alarm sounds blaring. We had a brief encounter with a security guard—"She's not a thief!"—and then stood in line (amazing how many people are out shopping at 10 P.M.) to pay for our purchases. When we finally made it to the front, the checkout clerk peeked inside the carrier, and said, "Oh, look at that gorgeous cat! Won't you need some grooming equipment? A scratch pole? We're offering a fifteen percent discount if you sign up for our Visa card, and here's some information about our new pet insurance policy. . . . It covers most vet bills—"

"No, thank you," I said, holding my mother by the hand.

"And do you want to include that adorable cap?" asked the clerk, pointing to my mother's other hand, which held a little hat—a red cat hat with holes for the ears and strings to tie under the chin.

"No, she doesn't. . . ." From her carrier, Beatrice let out a snarling "me-OW," as if I'd insulted her, and it was clear from my mother's tears that we wouldn't be leaving without the cap. The total came to $104.97, including $15 for the hat.

Back at the condo I helped my mother into her nightgown (no shower; she was too exhausted) and to bed, then set up my bathroom for the cat. "For the first couple of days, until she seems comfortable around you," Tony had advised, "keep her in a small room—I guess a bathroom would be best. You can bring her out for an hour or two, but let her have the security of the smaller space. Feed her there, and keep her litter box there. Let her have something soft to sleep on, like an old blanket."

So I gave my bathroom over to Beatrice, watched while she ate her dinner—tentatively at first, then with a rush of hunger. I closed the door, fell into bed without brushing my teeth, and slept hard—it must have been at least a couple of hours—until I heard a piercing howl. Beatrice was thrashing around in the toilet bowl. ("Don't forget to close the lid until she gets used to your place," Tony had said.) I toweled her off, let her follow me to the kitchen for some water, but when I tried to coax her back into the bathroom she'd have none of it. She jumped onto my bed. "Okay," I said, "just for tonight." I turned on my side and after a few minutes she settled in the space behind my knees.

"So, that must have been nice," says Gina, "all that purring and everything."

"Except she woke up at five." That rough tongue, and those huge eyes so close to mine.

"She probably wanted to play," says Gina. "Where is she, by the way?"

"At home. Mom loves her, and Delores didn't bitch too much."

Actually, Delores wasn't happy about the cat at all. "I thought you was a *real* lawyer," she'd said. "For people, I mean."

"What?" I was trying to revive myself with a third cup of coffee.

"First there was that dog, and now . . . *this*. What next, a possum?"

"I was appointed by the probate judge. I'm supposed to find her a good home."

"I thought probate was about dead people's money," she said.

"This cat inherited a lot of money."

Delores's eyes brightened. "If I keep the cat, do I get the money?"

"It's not that simple. But if you help me out for a couple of days, I'll make it up to you."

Delores has never had a pet. After her husband Charlie died, I'd made the mistake of suggesting she get a dog.

"You think some *animal* is gonna take the place of my Charlie?" she'd protested. "Besides, I keep a clean house." But she thinks I've forgotten that. "Look here, this cat likes me." Sure enough, Beatrice is rubbing her back against Delores's thigh. "This black girl knows a sister when she sees one!"

I spend an hour drafting a response to Derwood Carter's settlement proposal. This is something I could usually do in about half an hour, my brain darting along, but this morning I even stumble over the salutation. "Dear Judge Carter" would be respectful, but does it lend him an undeserved superiority? After all, he's chosen to represent himself, so he's his own lawyer, not a judge who can overrule me. But *Dear Derwood* invites familiarity, inviting him to cross the professional line. Hadn't he once called me back into his chambers after a trial to give me "a few pointers," closed the door, then asked me if I'd like to join him for drinks at his hotel? I was stunned—not at the realization that he was coming on to me, because I knew his reputation, but that he was so blatant, so infuriatingly sure that he could do this and get away with it. I should have reported him to the Judicial

Conduct Commission. Instead I said, "I don't want to keep you any longer, Your Honor," and left. That was a long time ago, but I'm still angry at myself.

I'd like to write:

Dear Judge Carter,

Your wife and I have reviewed your proposal for settlement of the financial issues arising out of your marriage. Either you have a serious misunderstanding of South Carolina law on the division of marital property and alimony, or your misogyny has affected your judgment. My own experience with you, both in and out of your courtroom, has confirmed your reputation as a womanizer of the worst kind, one who preys on the opposite sex with an attitude of entitlement. Your wife has endured this behavior for years, until, with my assistance, she obtained proof of your adultery. . . . Your proposal is so absurd that it doesn't merit a response. You have a choice: Send a reasonable settlement proposal within two weeks of the date of this letter, or we will proceed with discovery and request a trial date. I would also suggest you retain an attorney, since it is clear to me that you need the advice of someone with experience in Family Court.

But of course that's not the letter I draft. The one I'll send to Natalie Carter for her approval is thoroughly professional, its tone dry, straightforward, drained of my loathing for her husband. It outlines her contributions as a homemaker, mother, and secretary for his law practice, and includes citations to some relevant cases. The demand of 50 percent of the marital property is standard for a long marriage like this, and the request for alimony is just as reasonable. There's little chance he'll accept the offer, or anything close, but I'll send it so that later I can tell the trial judge, *Yes, Your Honor, we made a serious attempt to settle this case early on. Judge Carter rejected it, and we had no choice but to litigate. I believe we're entitled to an award of attorney's fees.*

Gina brings me a cup of coffee—a rare gesture, and not something I've ever asked her to do—along with a stack of phone messages and a file. "Don't forget the child neglect case this afternoon. That poor baby—"

"I thought the father got a continuance."

"He did. That was two weeks ago."

"It's not on my calendar."

"You're looking at November. This is December. If you'd keep your calendar on your iPhone, it would be a lot easier. But don't worry, I've got the file ready to go."

"You're wonderful, Gina."

"You don't have to be sarcastic."

"I'm not being sarcastic."

"I know you're still pissed off about the cat," she says.

"Just don't take on any more animal cases without asking me, okay?" I open my desk drawer. "But enough about that. Here's something for you."

She opens the envelope. "Wow. I wasn't expecting this much of a bonus."

"I couldn't do this job without you, and we had a good year."

"Thanks. But what's this?"

"The College of Charleston course catalogue. Check out the night courses."

"It would take me forever."

"Six years, maybe."

"I'd be fifty-six. What's the point?"

"You have to have a college degree before you can go to law school."

She laughs. "That's another three years! Who wants to hire a sixty-year-old lawyer?"

"Maybe *another* sixty-year-old lawyer."

"I'll think about it. By the way, I made the appointment for you, with Gail Sims."

"Who?"

"The woman who takes care of the Mackay plantation. You're meeting her tomorrow at noon, at the house. I've got directions in the file. . . . It's really out in the boonies. Oh, and I almost forgot. Mr. Hart called, said he wondered if you'd like to watch Sherman for a while on Saturday, something about putting their house up for sale. I told him I was sorry, I'd love to do it, but I have the first session with my personal trainer. And you'll have your hands full with your mom and the cat. . . . Hey, you're disappointed, aren't you!"

"Don't be silly, he's just a dog!" But the moment I say this I want to take it back. Sherman looks back at me—black eyes behind heavy brows—from the framed photo on my desk.

"Liar. You keep that picture there like he's an old boyfriend or something. Maybe the vet should be jealous. Just think," she says, "if the Harts hadn't reconciled, maybe you could have kept him."

"He's better off with them. I'm not very good at long-term relationships."

The truth is, I've been successful at only one long-term relationship: my twenty-five years with the law. My office is my real home. There's nothing grand about it, nothing like those oak-paneled lawyers' quarters with Persian rugs and expensive antique furnishings that announce to all who enter: "The firm of Venerable, August, and Esteemed has prospered here for three generations." I've rented it for ten years now, and because I'm an easy tenant (I know how to deal with a blocked toilet) the landlord has been reasonable about rent increases. I have a reception area that houses Gina's desk, a printer-copier, some file cabinets, and four chairs; a bathroom that also accommodates the coffeemaker and a shelf for supplies; a conference room that doubles as a library; and, at the end of the hall, my own office, big enough for my desk, a sofa, and two comfortable chairs.

It's not a perfect situation—third floor, an elevator that rattles and shimmies, no parking for clients. On the hottest summer days, the air-conditioning's inadequate. If I moved to the suburbs, West Ashley or Mt. Pleasant, I could have a lot more space for less money, maybe even buy a building of my own, but I like being two blocks from the courthouse and having the old city all around me. It gives me a sense of perspective. I have a framed photo on my office wall of Charleston after the Civil War—"The War Between the States," my mother calls it—with a view of Meeting Street looking south toward Broad. The devastation is horrible: buildings blown apart, rubble everywhere. When I've had an especially tough day I look at those ruins and remind myself that it could be a lot worse.

This afternoon, like every afternoon, the ruins are in the Family Court. This court is always about crumbling families—except for adoptions, when everyone is happy—but today the collapse seems total. This is DSS day, when two of the six courtrooms are set aside for the Department of Social Services to prosecute abuse and neglect cases. The waiting rooms are crammed with parents. The best of them are only adolescents themselves, who have no clue how to take care of a child. For a few of these, the system—a warning from the judge, parenting classes, monthly visits from the social worker—may work the way it's supposed to, but then there are the repeat offenders: the mother who leaves her toddler locked in the closet while she runs out for cigarettes, the father who smacks his kid hard enough to leave bruises. For these there are no easy fixes. Remove the child from the mom, and he's bounced from foster home to foster home. Give the dad a second chance, and tomorrow's headline may be a judge's nightmare.

Like every lawyer who practices in Family Court, I do my share of these pro bono cases. I'm searching the room for my client when the clerk calls the case: *"Department of Social Services vs. Tina White and Alfred Driggers."* It's a neglect case. Someone called DSS to report that the baby had been left alone. By the time the police arrived the mother had returned, but when DSS sent a social worker in to investigate, he found that the baby was seriously underweight.

I met with Tina White a week ago. She was an hour late for the appointment. "Missed my ride," she said. I studied her as she answered my questions: thin, pale hands trembling, her face much older than her eighteen years. I'd seen faces like this before. No, she said, she didn't use drugs, didn't drink "except a few beers now and then." The father "don't come around much 'cause I bug him about the child support." She admitted leaving the baby alone "for just half an hour while I walked to the grocery store. I didn't want to wake him up 'cause he had a bad night, bawling his head off." No, she had no idea why the baby, three months old, wasn't gaining weight. "He throws up a lot, though. My mother says I was the same way." While she sat in my office I called the clinic, made an appointment for her to take the child in the next day, got her to sign a medical release, explained what would happen at the hearing. "They can't take him away from me," she said before she left, tears trailing down her cheeks. "They got no right."

And now she doesn't show up for court. I do the best I can. "Your Honor, she lives in McClellanville. She doesn't have a car or a telephone. I'm sure she's on her way; if Your Honor could take the next case on the docket until . . ." But I don't sound convincing, even to myself. The father hasn't shown up either—undoubtedly he's afraid of going to jail for nonpayment of child support. The guardian *ad litem* for the baby, a young lawyer who's pro bono like me, has no choice but to agree with the department's request for temporary custody, and the judge orders DSS to pick up the child immediately and place him in foster care.

None of this is your fault, I tell myself as I ride the elevator down to the first floor, where I can at least escape the overheated courthouse. It's almost dark, time to get home to relieve Delores. I'm thinking about what we'll have for dinner when I hear a familiar voice. "So, you're not speaking to me?" It's Joe, my ex.

"Sorry, I didn't see you."

"Bad day?"

"A DSS hearing. The usual. Depressing."

"You okay otherwise?"

"No complaints," I say. Since the dog case we've abided by the terms of an unspoken agreement: We won't talk about anything personal—his marriage, my relationship with Tony.

"Heard you got a cat," he says, his smile a little wicked. I hate the smile because, despite my best efforts, I still love it. "I promise I had nothing to do with that, but think about it—wouldn't you rather deal with a cat than your usual client?" Again the smile. "Take care, Sally. And if I don't see you again before Christmas, have a good one. My best to your mother."

As I walk back to my office it starts to drizzle, a fine mist fracturing the lights of rush-hour traffic. A car slams on brakes, just missing a man who's jaywalking. He stops mid-street, curses, loses hold of his umbrella, his briefcase. I retrieve the umbrella, hand it to him. I recognize him—he practices in one of the big firms—but can't remember his name.

"Thanks," he says. He brushes the rain off his coat. "You see that?

She was going too damn fast!" We part ways. No need to remind him that he was jaywalking, that it wasn't all her fault.

When I left Joe, he said some things that cut to the quick, like *You're never going to find anyone who loves you like I do. You're not an easy woman to live with, you know!* But looking back, I'm amazed that he remained relatively calm. In fact, the more I think about it—and I do, often—the more I realize that I needed him to be angrier. Instead, he seemed helpless, accepting my decision as passively as he did the life that his family had designed for him. His choice of me as his wife was the one exception to this pattern of acquiescence. It made no sense.

This is one of those afternoons, though, when it's best *not* to try to make sense of things: A cat with three million dollars, a baby on his way to foster care. Love, and the mess we make of it.

The Beatrice Box

———◆———

With her usual efficiency, Gina has sorted the paper contents of Lila Mackay's box into separate notebooks: "Vet bills," "Notes," "Letters," "Miscellaneous."

The oldest vet bill is from seven years ago, "Core vaccines, kitten series $45.00," the most recent three months ago, "Office visit, hip dysplasia. Recommend weight loss. $50.00." Except for the occasional bout of roundworms and ear mites, Beatrice has been a healthy cat. There's a letter dated shortly before Mrs. Mackay's death: "This office will be closing on December 31 due to my retirement. Unless you notify us that you wish your pet's records sent elsewhere, we will transfer them to Dr. Harriett McCoy in Rantowles. We have enclosed her card for your convenience."

The notes are more interesting, page after page on white stationery, written in black (I imagine the fountain pen, the jar of ink), a cursive that in the first thirty or so pages is almost too perfect, the lines evenly spaced and very straight. Later the handwriting is shaky, the letters larger; the lines drift upward. In the final pages there are frequent corrections, words and phrases scratched out or put in parentheses with notes above them: "Not right word," "Need better metaphor," "Silly?"

Most of the notes are in first person and seem to be a sort of diary, though one only sporadically kept:

I spent most of the day by the fireplace. Too cold for our usual walk. She didn't go out, either; catching up on her correspondence. Billy stopped to pick up Gail's check. (She does the work, why does he get the check?)

Another entry:

Delightful afternoon on the piazza. Not too hot. There's something hypnotic about the Spanish moss swaying back and forth in the breeze. She's nearby, reading. We are such different creatures, but alike in our inability to trust anyone completely.

Who, I wonder, is this other woman? Is she still alive? Why wouldn't Mrs. Mackay have chosen her as the cat's caregiver? But the next note explains it:

Caught a mouse this morning. Was having fun until she took it away. "Not on your diet!" she says.

Mrs. Mackay is writing as if she's Beatrice, the cat. Maybe she *was* crazy after all.

I skip to the letters. There are carbon copies of letters written on an old typewriter whose lower-case *b* and *t* are off-center. One to the Highway Commission opposing a proposal to widen the highway onto the island, which will require removing some oak trees: "We who live on Edisto consider these trees our cherished friends. Some are three hundred years old. Would it not be wiser and kinder for us to slow down, rather than to cut them down?" A letter to the editor of the Columbia paper, from 1999: "The time has come for us to acknowledge that continuing to fly the Confederate flag at the State House is not done 'to honor our history' but to preserve a symbol which is offensive to many. At best, this is an appalling display of bad manners; at worst, it is deliberately cruel."

Another, from 1990: "My husband loved The Citadel. He served on its Board of Governors and gave generously to support scholarship students. Since his death I have tried to match his generosity, but I can no longer give to an institution which refuses to admit women. When you see fit to change your policy in this regard, I will resume my annual gifts." Gina has stuck a note on this one: *What does this have to do with the cat?*

After the carbon copies there's another stack of letters, undated, all in the same handwriting. The earliest is dated almost thirty years ago:

> *Dear Lila,*
>
> *I have given our recent conversation much thought. Of course it was distressing to hear that you are so unhappy. I should not have added to that unhappiness by saying what I did, but surely you know that my feelings about your current predicament are complicated by our history. Whatever you decide to do, please know that I shall always be your devoted friend. Stop by the store when you're next in Charleston—I've made some improvements.*
>
> *Fondly, Simon*
>
> *P.S. Under the circumstances, you should probably resist your usual urge to file this away in your "archives."*

I scan the next four letters from Simon. Nothing more about her unhappiness.

Dear Lila,

I will have to decline your invitation to lunch next week, as I am temporarily confined to the apartment. The surgeon (a woman, very smart but, like you, a little dictator) has decreed that I rest, lest I ruin my ankle completely.

So pleased to hear about your new friend. I assume Beatrice likes Dante? (Don't be so snooty about her lack of pedigree. I thought you were more egalitarian than that.) May she be as loyal a companion to you as McCavity has been to me.

By the way, I'm sure you'll hear, if you haven't already, that the bookstore is closing. Soon King Street will be nothing but expensive shops, the same national chains you can find in any sizable town. Shall I venture to say this is one more sign that the world is going to hell, or do I just sound like a bitter old man?

Fondly,

S.

Precious

———※———

"Most cats don't travel well," Tony had said, and Beatrice seems determined to prove him right, her high-pitched cries starting the minute I put her in the car, becoming louder at each intersection—she doesn't like moving, but she doesn't like stopping, either—as I drive south on Highway 17 toward Edisto.

"Settle down, honey," I say, and she glares at me through the holes in the carrier as if to say, *Don't call me 'honey.'* But as we leave the heavy traffic behind and cross the Wallace River she's calmer, her complaints less dramatic, and by the time we turn onto Toogoodoo Road, she's quiet.

Does she know we're headed toward Edisto Island? I remember reading about a lost cat who walked two hundred miles to find home. My sense of direction can't compare: I frequently get lost when I leave the Charleston peninsula, despite instructions from the GPS lady (I finally had to disable the thing; she was driving me crazy). "The reason you get lost," my ex, Joe, once said, "is that you always want to be somewhere else." He was right: I was always imagining what it would be like to live somewhere else. Out West, I'd fantasize, or Alaska. "Or maybe you don't really want to live someplace else," he said, "you want to *be* someone else." And he was right again. "Remember, even if you manage to get a change of venue, you're still going to be the same old self!"

Edisto is the kind of place, only an hour from Charleston, where I can imagine being someone else. The state highway winds through the country: woodland and marsh, farms, a few houses. Sometimes the road seems about to disappear into the marsh and I'm sure I'm really lost this time, but then I recognize the intersection. Beatrice, on the seat beside me, is lying down but alert, her head erect. When I make the left onto Highway 174 she lets out a long satisfied "meow," as if to say: *Yes, I really* am *going home!*

It's been years since I've driven out here—the last time wasn't long after my divorce from Joe, when Frank McGill took me to a New Year's Day oyster roast. I'd accepted the invitation only because Frank, a fellow public defender, insisted he was just trying to cheer me up. I wasn't ready to start dating again, and wondered if I'd ever be. But at just about this point in the drive—the bridge over the Edisto River—Frank confided that he'd had a crush on me since law school. Poor thing, his wooing skills were about on par with his courtroom skills, his argument pathetically sincere but hopeless. I did my best to state my case without crushing him: *It has nothing to do with you, Frank, I'm just not ready.*

By the time we arrived at the party I was desperate to disappear into the crowd. I found a place at one of the tables with people I didn't know. We stood around in the cold, stamping our feet and poking around in the pile of picked-over oysters and waiting for the next load to be shoveled onto the table. When they came I busied myself prying a big one open, finding the slit between the halves of the sharp shell, twisting the knife until the thing revealed its glistening meat. Shucking oysters is dangerous business even with gloves, and since I was a determined vegetarian, I was violating my principles. I remember the pain as the knife slipped, jabbing my wrist just above the glove.

There was a lot of blood, and the hostess insisted I come inside the house to clean the wound, and then—I should have known he might be there—Joe was next to me, his arm touching my elbow. "Probably won't need stitches," he said, "but you ought to get some antibiotic on it." There was a woman with him, one of those dainty creatures who manage to look petite even in multiple layers of heavy clothing. "Sally, you remember Susan Harmon?" I nodded dumbly, closed the bathroom door, and cried while I let the hot water run over the cut. I convinced Frank to take me home early. "I have a terrible headache," I said.

I did have a headache, but it wasn't from the pain of the wound. I'd been undone by seeing Joe with another woman. It was totally foreseeable, of course. He was young, good-looking, affable, an associate in his family's venerable Charleston firm. He was still living in our apartment, but would soon, with his parents' help, buy a place of his own a couple of blocks away from their house on Church Street. As far as they were concerned he'd made only one mistake in his life, and that was to marry me, that strange ungainly girl from upstate, who was definitely not, as they would say, "our kind of people." She was smart, yes, but why on earth did she want to work at the public defender's office? Thank God she'd done him the favor of leaving him—after only a year, can you imagine!—though everyone said she'd lost her mind. If she thought she'd ever find a husband better than their Joe, she had another think coming.

And now I look for the turnoff to Oak Bluff Plantation Road. ("It's a dirt road, on your right, about half a mile after you pass the Presbyterian church," said Gail Sims, the caretaker, who's meeting me at the house. "The road'll wind around and you'll see a coupla trailers and then an old store and not much after that you'll come to the gate. Just push it open—it's not locked." As we pass through the gate the cat lifts her chin, looks straight ahead. She can't see what I see—the glimpse of gray-white behind the row of oaks, the red roof against the clear sky—but she knows where we're going.

The house isn't as large as I'd imagined, and badly needs painting. It seems very plain, boxlike, until I realize I've approached the back side of the house. I follow a brick walkway around to the front, and then I can see the glory of the place: the view from the bluff overlooking the river. There's a wide piazza running the length of the house on the main floor, reachable by a long, wide flight of stairs.

I'm looking up the stairs at what must be the front door, dreading the thought of having to lug Beatrice in her carrier, when a young woman appears at ground level, right in front of me, as if she's come from nowhere.

"Oh, precious!" she says to the cat. "I've been missing you!" And to me: "I'm Gail. Come on in." She gestures toward what seems to be a basement door, under the stairs. "We can talk down here if that's okay—save you the climb. It's kind of a mess upstairs, anyway." She leads me into a large, musty-smelling kitchen, one countertop completely covered with magazines and newspapers. "Watch your head. In the old days this part of the house was just used for storage," she explains, "but Lila turned it into an apartment for herself, turned the storeroom into this kitchen, and she stayed down here most of the time. This room over here," she says as we cross a narrow hallway, "is where she did her writing. Lila, she was always writing. I told her she should get a real desk—you know, with drawers to put stuff—but she just wouldn't hear of moving her papers and things off that old table. I did my best to help her keep things straight, but she wouldn't let me touch them." Indeed, there are piles of papers on the long table behind the sofa. But despite its clutter, the room is inviting and warm, with a fire going strong in the fireplace. "Billy says this is the only part of the house that's livable."

"Billy?"

"My fiancé. We been together a while now." She looks about thirty, boyish, her wheat-colored hair cut short, her jeans clean but showing some wear and tear. "He works on the shrimp boats." She moves some magazines off the sofa, gives the cushion a swat. Dust rises, swirls in the light from the fire. "You can set right here. Sorry the place is such a mess. She wouldn't let anybody touch it while she was alive, but I shoulda come down here and cleaned up after she passed. I guess I—I just couldn't get it through my head that she wasn't coming back."

"Don't worry about it," I say, "this shouldn't take long."

"Time to let you out of jail," Gail says to Beatrice, opening the door to the carrier. "Come here, you precious thing, come to Gail." She sits on the wide hearth across from me and the cat settles in her lap. "There! You know where you belong, don't you, precious?" The fire crackles behind her.

"So," I take a notepad out of my purse, "you understand why I'm here?"

"I heard about the will."

"Actually, it's a trust."

"Well, whatever it is, I heard it's a lot of money. Don't it beat all?" She strokes Beatrice under the chin, which the cat clearly enjoys. "Who'da thought she was so loaded?"

"Did Mrs. Mackay discuss the terms of the trust with you before she died?"

"She sure didn't. Lila was real private about her money."

"So, how did you learn about it?" I ask.

"Word kind of gets around. I was knocked right off my rocker when I heard. I mean, you just look around." Her hand, dirt under the fingernails, sweeps through the air. "Does it look like she had a lotta money? Anyway, I don't know much about them other two, you know, that she put in the will or the whatever, but you can best believe that me and Beatrice here, we've always been buddies. Just like Lila—Miz Mackay—and me, we was good buddies."

"I can tell she likes you." Beatrice's purr is loud enough to hear over the whistle of the hot air going up the flue. "Would you be willing to care for the cat, then?"

"Oh, sure. I'd give her a good home. Billy and me got a three-bedroom mobile over there off Oyster Factory Road, which will be fine until we can build—"

"But you understand that under the terms of the trust, the caretaker must live here with the cat."

"That just don't seem necessary," she says. "A cat don't need a big ole place like this, with the ghost and all."

"Ghost?"

"I never did see him, but Lila did. She always said she wasn't afraid of him—said it was a friendly ghost, but a ghost is a ghost as far as I'm concerned."

"So you wouldn't want to live here?"

"Like I said, it don't seem necessary, but then again, what am I saying?" She stops herself, biting her lip. "Billy and me, we'll do anything we have to do to take care of this precious animal!"

"How old is the house?"

"Plenty old. Like, about 1800, I think."

"You work on the island, is that right?"

"Part-time over there at the nursery."

"You take care of children?"

She laughs. "Oh, no! It's the *plant* kind of nursery. That's how I got to know Lila. She'd come every now and then to buy stuff for her garden—it's not much now, but you should see it in spring and summer—and one time we got to talking about cats, and I told her about my cats and she said she needed somebody to look after Beatrice when she'd go into Charleston overnight, and I said sure, be happy to. And then I started helping her out with the grass-mowing and the garden, and I got really close to her."

"How did she die?"

"Cancer. Kept that a secret except for me and Billy. Wouldn't do chemo, though from what she told me, it probably wouldn't have done any good anyway. In the end it was a heart attack. A blessing, I guess. Right out there in the rose garden. She loved her roses. Her roses, her writing, and Beatrice here. That's what kept her going."

"How many cats do you have?"

"Two."

"So when you'd take care of Beatrice, did you bring your cats here?"

"Billy stayed with them. Lila—Miz Mackay—wanted Beatrice to stay at home, so I'd come over here for a night or two when she went into Charleston. And Billy don't like this house, anyway. I'm not, you know, suspicious . . . superstitious or whatever, but he was really freaked out when I told him about the ghost."

"But I thought you said you hadn't seen the ghost." I look down at my notes so that she won't see the smile that's tugging at the corners of my mouth.

"No, but like I said, Lila told me about him. She always said he wouldn't hurt a flea, but Billy—"

"So you'd prefer not to live here?"

"Not unless we have to. Like I said, Beatrice would be fine at our place, wouldn't you, precious?" Gail strokes the cat's back. Beatrice's eyes are closed, her body relaxed. "She'd get along fine with Sponge-Bob and SquarePants. They behave themselves pretty good most of the time. . . . Anyway, I think I could do as good a job as anybody, with Beatrice, I mean. Does the will or whatever say we *definitely* got to live here?"

"The trust states . . . let me see, I have a copy . . . that 'the chosen caregiver shall reside with Beatrice, during Beatrice's lifetime, at my home . . . and shall endeavor to provide Beatrice with the same life-style, routine, and emotional environment as she has become accustomed to in my care.' What do you think that means?"

"Doesn't make a whole lot of sense. I thought 'environment' is about the outside, but Beatrice never did spend much time outside. I know the 'routine' thing is important, though, for a cat."

"What's her routine?" I'm taking notes: *Beatrice comfortable with Gail. Gail's affection for her seems genuine.*

"She likes to sleep with Lila—I mean, before—but if I take care of her I guess she'll sleep with me and Billy."

"That wouldn't upset *your* cats?"

"Oh, they'll be okay after everybody gets adjusted. You want to see upstairs? Everybody always wants to see the upstairs, it being so historic and all."

"Sure," I say, though I don't really care for a tour, "but let me finish up with my questions."

"I guess that's what lawyers do," she says. "They ask a ton of questions!"

"We were talking about the cat's routine."

"Right. She wakes up pretty early, wants something to eat. She'll walk around her empty bowl until you give her something, acts like she's starving to death! Lila would always say, wait until supper-time, feed her once a day, but as fat as she is—the cat, I mean—looks like she broke her own rule, so when I had her—I gotta tell the truth—sometimes I spoiled her, gave her a little something in the morning. And then she'd pretty much sleep the rest of the day, unless it was story time."

"Story time?"

"Yeah, I know it sounds crazy, but Lila would read her stories. There's one of the books right there, beside you." Atop a stack of newspapers there's an old book, with a brown leather cover, faded gold letters on the binding: *Aesop's Fables*. "It's the darnedest thing, I could swear Beatrice understands it. The one about a cat and a fox— that's her favorite."

"Maybe she just liked the sound of Mrs. Mackay's voice. . . . You said you work part-time. What about Billy?"

"When he's not shrimping, he takes people out on fishing char- ters. Right now things are kinda slow. . . . Let me show you upstairs." She's insistent. "Kinda run-down, but interesting . . . all those antiques and all."

"Okay, sure."

"We'll just let Beatrice stay right here where it's warm. Don't worry, she'll be fine. Won't you, precious?" The cat opens her yellow eyes briefly as she's transferred from lap to hearth, then closes them again.

I follow Gail up the wooden staircase to the main floor. She moves with a self-assured, muscular grace. It's hard to believe she's afraid of anything, much less a ghost. "You see what I mean?" We've reached the landing, which is really a central hall. "In the old days they built the houses like this—two big rooms on each floor. The kitchen used to be in a separate building, but it burned down a long time ago. That there used to be the living room, I guess, but Lila only used it when she had company. Like I said, in the last few years she spent most of her time downstairs."

The room is huge, with twelve-foot ceilings. Between the two long windows overlooking the river there's a floor-to-ceiling mirror crowned with gold-painted cherubs; on the opposite wall, a fireplace with a marble mantelpiece. From the chandelier, cracks spread out across the ceiling; in one corner a large chunk of plaster has fallen away, revealing the lath skeleton underneath. Matching sofas—Victorian, I'm guessing—face each other around the fireplace. One's covered with books and papers, the other draped with an old blanket. Along one wall, surrounding both north-facing windows, are glass-covered bookcases crammed with books.

Gail points to the missing piece of ceiling: "It's kind of a maintenance nightmare, this place. Like I said, I can do a lot, but she wouldn't let me touch the plaster, said it needed a specialist. I found a guy in Charleston who could do it but she said he was too high. You know old people—I guess even the ones that got plenty of money, they don't want to part with it. So the house just kind of got away from her. I think that's part of the reason she spent most of her time downstairs—that, and she didn't have to deal with the stairs. She even got to where she slept down there, on the sofa, so she wouldn't have to climb up to the bedroom. This over here," she continues, leading me back across the hall, "is the dining room, but she quit using it a long time ago." The table is probably twenty feet long, covered with papers and books. "You want to see the bedrooms?"

We go up another flight of stairs. The banister shakes a little as I steady myself. "Wow," I say when we get to the top, the landing above the central hall below. The view from the huge window is spectacular: down the wide lawn, maybe a hundred yards, to a point where a dock stretches across the marsh to the river.

"You can catch pretty good crabs off that dock. She used to love to pick crabs. Used to eat them all the time. Weeks would go by and she'd eat nothing but crabs and cole slaw! I used to help her with the net, but then she got too wobbly to walk out there. I said, I'll do it myself, but in the last coupla years she quit eating them anyway, said she couldn't bear to see them go into the boiling water. . . . Anyway, if you look way, way out there you can see the ocean. Over here's her bedroom, but like I said, when it got near the end she didn't get up here much." This room is the same size as the living room below, with a high four-poster bed. "She still kept most of her clothes in that chifforobe. There's some fancy stuff in there, but kind of old-fashioned, like those long white gloves ladies used to wear, know what I mean? You want to see?"

"No, thanks." I feel like an intruder already.

"And around here's the bathroom. . . . There's one in the basement, too, which is the one she mostly used. . . . And this"—we're on the other side of the house now—"is the guest room. Kind of a wreck, so I guess it'd been a while since she had anybody spend the night." Another tall bed, this one covered with more books and papers.

"Watch yourself going down these steps. . . . They built these a long time ago, when people's feet were a lot smaller! You have any more questions, you just let me know. Like I say, Billy and me, we'd be tickled to take care of Beatrice. Speaking of which, where are you, precious?"

Beatrice isn't on the hearth. She isn't on the sofa or in the kitchen.

"Precious!" Gail yells, and when that fails to produce the cat, she begs: "Come here, kitty-kitty. Come to Gail." Nothing.

"Maybe she snuck past us on the stairs," I suggest.

But when Gail opens the door to the backyard, there's Beatrice—and she's not alone.

It's in My Blood

———◆———

"idn't mean to scare you," he says, grinning—an unnatural grin that displays his prominent incisors, a rim of his upper gum. He's a huge man, I'm guessing over six feet, with massive shoulders and a neck so thick, his blocklike head seems too small for his body. He has the red nose of a drinker, a purplish web of veins spreading to his cheeks. The cat squirms in the crook of his arm, her back legs wedged between his arm and his chest.

"Oh, hi, Randall," says Gail. "We were looking for her! Watch out, she's going to—" But Beatrice is already clawing her way up his chest, onto his shoulder, and in one spectacular burst of determination she leaps away from him, almost flying, landing behind him in the grass.

"Damn!" he says, "Got a temper on her, doesn't she?" And again that forced grin as he steps toward me, extends a hand. "Randall Mackay. You must be the law-yer." He says "lawyer" like it's a dirty word.

"I was just leaving," I say. The cat peers at us through the branches of an oleander, wary.

"Come here, precious," says Gail. "Come to mama."

"No need to run away," says Randall, to me. "Gail will tell you I'm harmless." He smiles, heavy black eyebrows arching, one higher than the other. He's outfitted for hunting: a green-gray camouflage jacket and matching pants, boots. "You must be a mighty busy lawyer. I left messages."

I look him straight in the eye. "I *am* very busy, but I should have some time next week, if you'd like to call again and make an appointment."

"Well, *you're* here and *I'm* here," he says, "so we might as well take advantage of this, uh, opportunity." Gail has cajoled the cat into coming out from behind the oleander, has her safe in her arms. "You wouldn't mind watching the cat while we talk, would you, Gail? Maybe she'd like to spend a little time outside while—"

"She don't really like it much out here," Gail replies. "Cats, you know, they like to be inside."

"Fine," he says, "the law-yer and I, we'll go on up to the living room and you and our furry friend can stay down here." He opens the door, stands back, and gestures for us to go in. "Ladies first."

I remember what Judge Clarkson said: *Steer clear of him.* But I've been in situations much scarier than this, like when I was a young public defender doing my own investigation on a murder case, knocking on doors in a bad North Charleston neighborhood, asking lots of questions; or interviewing a new client at the county jail, sitting across the table in a tiny room listening to him tell me how he hadn't killed anybody—*You can't kill a witch. She's the devil's handmaiden, put a curse on me, put a curse on my daddy, too. You don't believe me? She's right there behind you, working her curse on you, too!* And there was the time, a couple of years ago, when I received four unsigned letters at my office, printed in a strange, cramped font, warning that I would be sorry if I continued to represent a local doctor in his divorce. That evening I left my office after a particularly stressful day, to find that all four tires on my car were flat. I suspected the doctor's wife—she had mental problems—but I couldn't prove she'd sent the letters.

"No problem," Gail says to Randall. "You all just take your time. Beatrice and I, we'll be fine."

I follow Randall up the staircase. "Look around," Randall says when we reach the living room. "You think this was a woman in her right mind? A fortune in stocks and bonds and she lived like this? Jesus." He shoves a pile of books off one of the sofas, lets them fall to the floor. "I'll get straight to the point. You don't need to take notes—it's not complicated." The sofa gives a little under his weight. "My mother was always a little nutty. Lived in her own world, with all these books, played like she was a real historian, writing articles mostly nobody published unless she supported the magazine. Wasn't much of a wife, couldn't hide her relief when my daddy died, though God knows he was good to her, gave her everything she wanted."

"Mr. Mackay," I say, "My role in this case is to—"

"I know what your role is. You really let old Judge Clarkson pass the buck to you, didn't you?"

"He's retiring soon, and apparently he's not in good health."

"He didn't want to deal with the cat," Randall Mackay says. "And frankly I can't understand why a successful law-yer like you would want to waste your time. . . . Anyway, as I was saying, my mother was always crazy, but in the last five years or so, that brain of hers went haywire. Burney Haynes—he was her law-yer—should have known that. I guess she must have paid him a bundle, so he didn't want to cross her."

"Are you alleging that your mother lacked the capacity to understand what she was doing?"

"Damn right I am."

"But apparently you believed she was capable of living out here all by herself?"

"We hired some people to stay with her. She fired them all. I should have had her declared incompetent, put her in a home."

"But you didn't."

"No, I just couldn't do it to her. She loved this place." His voice softens. "I guess you know something about how hard it is, when they get demented."

"What?"

"Your mother."

My whole body tenses. "How do you know about my mother?"

"Your ex—we hunt together sometimes."

"You know Joe?"

"Friend of a friend," he says. Again the grin, the arched eyebrows. "No need to get all huffy. I'm just pointing out that we have something in common. When it's your own mother, you don't think straight. But never mind all that, I have to protect myself now."

"Then you should hire a lawyer."

"I'd like to avoid that." he says.

"But I can't advise you, Mr. Mackay."

"I'm going to cut to the chase. If I contest this trust, we're going to use up a whole bunch of time and a whole bundle of money in unnecessary litigation. And at the end of all that, there'll be some kind of settlement, so why not just get right down to it? I'm willing to work a deal."

"My job is to choose the best caregiver for the cat. I'm not really concerned with—"

"But if I succeed in setting the trust aside," he says, arching his right eyebrow, "all this nonsense about the cat goes out the window."

"Again, Mr. Mackay, I can't advise you."

"But you can hear me out. The deal I propose is this: Let Gail keep the cat. She's a good kid, and her boyfriend's okay, too. Pay her that ridiculous salary, since that's what my mother wanted, but they don't need to live here in this house. Hell, they don't even want to. And in exchange I won't raise any objection to the trust. Everybody's happy."

"So *you* want to live here?"

"I'll get the property after the cat dies anyway."

"I don't think I have the authority to make a deal like that, even if I thought it was advisable," I explain. "My role as trust enforcer is to—"

"Oh, for God's sake, Judge Clarkson doesn't give a damn who gets the cat or where the cat lives. If he did, he'd be handling this himself. He just wants to wash his hands of the whole thing, because he knows how crazy my mother is . . . was."

"I need to get back to Charleston, but I'll think about what you said."

"I trust you will . . . no pun intended."

"Just one question: What if I continue with my investigation, and I determine that one of the others—the librarian, or the nephew in New York—would be willing to move here, and would make the best caregiver for Beatrice?"

"Then the deal is off. Look." He's turning red, and though it's cold in the room, his forehead is damp with perspiration. "My mother thought Gail would take good care of the cat, otherwise she wouldn't be on the list. And Gail's willing to take the cat. Why make it more complicated? Or is it that you just want to rack up a bunch of hours on my mother's dime?"

"If you're going to challenge the trust, you'll need to hire a lawyer."

"I'll do whatever I have to do. This house isn't just a piece of real estate to me," he says. "My great-great-great-great-great grandfather built it. That's six generations. It's in my blood. Look, I like cats, but I'm not going to let some damn *animal* keep me from getting what's mine. Now," he says, standing up, "I don't want to take up any more of your time. You think it over, what I've said."

"I will, but I want to reiterate—"

"You law-yers like fancy words, don't you? You usually get, what, fifty dollars a word? So maybe for the fancy ones, you get a hundred, right?"

Just before he drives off he says, "Don't let anything happen to that cat, you hear?" His truck, a big shiny black one, roars away.

Beatrice doesn't want to part with Gail, or maybe she doesn't want to leave her warm spot by the fire. She complains mightily about getting back in her carrier. "Poor thing," says Gail, "she just got back home and now you're going to . . . And she hates the car. You sure you don't want to leave her with me?"

"I wish I could."

"Can't say as I understand all this legal stuff," she says.

"I have to interview two other people. But it shouldn't take long."

"I don't even know why she—Lila—even named them. That librarian lady—"

"Katherine Harleston?"

"Yeah, her. She's nice enough, but her husband's kind of, you know, a snobby-type Charleston person. I can't see him moving out here. And the nephew, he lives in New York. Only been down once to see her, since I started working out here, anyway."

"How long is that?"

"About five years. He's, you know . . ."

"No, tell me."

"I guess you'll see for yourself. Anyway, I just can't see him wanting to live down here."

"By the way, how did Randall know I'd be here today?"

"I guess my boyfriend—my fiancé, I mean—might have told him. They're friends."

"Where does Randall live?"

"Over on the front beach," she says. "Lila bought the house for him a while back, before the property values went through the roof."

"So he doesn't really need a place to live."

"He's just got a sentimental connection to this house, I guess."

"But if he and his mother didn't get along, I don't understand—"

"Randall's always been kind of a mystery," she says with a shrug.

I look at my watch. "Thanks for all the information, Gail—and the house tour. I'll be in touch."

"No problem," she says. "You take care of my precious Beatrice, okay?"

By the time I get back to my condo, I've come to a few conclusions:

—I don't drive well with a complaining cat in the car. (How did I go ten miles out of my way before I realized I'd made a wrong turn?)

—I don't trust Randall.

—Beatrice trusts Gail.

It's clear that Mrs. Mackay believed Gail would be an adequate caretaker for the cat. Despite my reservations about Randall, what would be so wrong with his proposal: Beatrice goes to live with Gail, who'll get $50,000 a year to take care of her. Randall gets the plantation free and clear and agrees not to challenge the trust. And—although I hate to admit I'm even taking this into consideration—I can rid myself of this cat.

Encumbrances

After I divorced Joe, I tried to reinvent myself. I'd failed at being a well-adjusted wife to a nicer-than-average husband; failed to appreciate what everyone else thought was my amazing good luck at being taken in by one of Charleston's most respected law firms—his family's; and failed at even that most basic biological function, baby-making. I gave up trying to explain to anyone but my best friend Ellen why I couldn't stay at the firm or why I'd left Joe, and no one but Ellen and Joe knew about the miscarriage. Most of my colleagues—though of course no one said this to my face—assumed there must be something really wrong with me, some fundamental defect of personality, an if not fatal at least very unfortunate character flaw.

I couldn't disagree with them. I never blamed Joe. "He's a wonderful guy," I'd say if pressed for an explanation, "we just weren't a good fit." And I never said anything negative about his family firm. After all, his father and his uncles had tried to accommodate me—I, the first female in the firm's 130-year history. "They couldn't have been nicer," I'd say, "but I missed my public interest work."

I now realize that my desire to reinvent myself arose out of distorted logic: If I was defective, I thought, I might as well be defective in an interesting way. If I had a character flaw, or more than one, I might as well *be* a character. I cut my hair very short, limited my wardrobe to black and neutral colors, eschewed makeup, even lipstick. I furnished my new apartment in minimalist style, with a white sofa, a black chair, a glass-topped dining table, and a bed. All my old furniture, the frayed but comfortable stuff, I put in storage. (I guess there was some frayed, comfortable part of me that needed to hang on to it.) I bought some cheap Rothko reproductions—his "black and gray" phase—and hung them on the walls. On the nights I didn't eat at home I sat by myself in a corner booth at Greens and Grains, an earnest vegan restaurant that soon went out of business. I bought expensive running shoes, started jogging and lost ten pounds, though I hadn't been overweight to begin with.

This was my misguided attempt at self-purification, the purging of everything Sally. "You're being too hard on yourself," said Ellen. "And—I hate to say this, but who the hell else is going to— that haircut is not at all flattering. Your ears are not your best feature."

"I don't have time for hair," I said. True, I'd been spending long hours trying to stay on top of my new caseload at the public defender's office, the mostly hopeless cases of the mostly guilty. But Ellen worked as hard as I did as an assistant solicitor, prosecuting child abusers and rapists, and somehow she managed to find time for regular appointments at the salon, not to mention a husband, a baby, and a well-kept house.

"I don't want any encumbrances," I said.

"Would a *rug* be too much of an encumbrance?" she asked, looking around my apartment living room. "Or maybe a coffee table?"

"I want to be really careful about my choices from now on," I explained. "I don't want to blithely accumulate things. That's what happens to people—they start accumulating things and before they know it they're up to their ears in stuff they don't need."

"Does 'stuff' include relationships?" Ellen's good at cross-examination.

"We were talking about furniture."

"I know, but don't you see what you're doing to yourself?"

"I'm trying to start over. A clean slate. Whatever I buy from now on will be the result of a deliberate and conscious choice—not just a bunch of stuff I've accumulated."

She laughed. "Wow, you're in worse shape than I thought! You're twenty-six years old, honey, still young, that's true, but *way* past the clean-slate stage. You can't just wipe out your past and start over as if it never happened."

She was right, of course. I needed a coffee table, preferably one I wouldn't mind putting my feet on—like the one in storage with the dents and scratches—for those nights I'd come home from court, beat. And I needed my old sofa back, with its paisley print that would graciously accommodate the drips from a coffee cup or the excess mustard from a hastily made sandwich. I needed my books and my cheap sagging bookcases and my stacks of old *New Yorkers*. The Rothko prints depressed me. I missed the Kandinsky reproduction with the red comet, though it was slightly faded, and even the lousy paintings I'd done in college when I imagined myself an artist.

Gradually all this stuff found its way back into my apartment and shared the space with my new purchases. It was clear to any observer that Sally-the-Decorator had a split personality, equal parts ascetic and eclectic. And now I seem to have accumulated, deliberately or not, a great deal more than mismatched furniture: I've got a boyfriend who wants to be a husband, an ex-husband I can't quite get out of my heart, and an aging mother with all her accoutrements. Plus a cat.

This evening when I get home, my mother is in the act of sorting out some stuff of her own. "She's been packing a suitcase," says Delores. "Says she's going to 'the plantation.' You think she means that place—Middleton?—where I took her a while back?"

"Could be, or maybe she heard me say something about going out to Edisto."

"How was it? Nice house?"

"It's seen better days."

"Like with a hundred slaves?"

"You know that's not what I mean."

"I got some cousins on Edisto, live over there behind the AME church. Seems like the jungle to me, snakes and all that. And what's an old lady gonna do if she needs to get to the hospital? Takes an hour on those curvy roads, and you can't go too fast or you'll end up in the swamp. Anyway, she must have been plenty lonely."

"Mrs. Mackay had Beatrice to keep her company." Delores eyes the carrier, the creature inside. "That cat don't look too happy."

"She hates the car, but she'll calm down. Did Mom have supper?"

"A cup of split pea soup and some corn bread. I had to push it on her—she was all riled up, bound and determined to pack that suitcase. . . . You want me to stay a little longer so you can have a few minutes to yourself? There's plenty of soup; I left it on the stove. And the corn bread's still warm."

"No, you go ahead, unless you want to stay and have some supper yourself." I've noticed that since Charlie's death, Delores doesn't seem in her usual hurry to get home.

"That would be nice. I'll make us a salad, too."

Mom is back in her bedroom, the suitcase open on the bed, her arms full of clothes. "Mom, where are you going?"

She turns around, her eyes darting, her mouth and jaw set in that expression I've seen before. She's forgotten where she is, yet she's determined to go somewhere else. She doesn't answer, but folds the clothes, arranges them in the suitcase, except for one dress. She lifts it up, shakes it out so that the long skirt falls to the floor. "Maybe this one should go on a hanger," she says.

I put my hand on her shoulder, speak as gently as I can, "Mom, where are you going?"

"To the party. The party in the country."

"It must be a really fancy party." The dress is gorgeous, emerald-green taffeta. I can't remember the last time she wore it, or where.

"We're staying for the weekend," she says.

"Who are you going with?"

"Frank doesn't want to go, so Ed Shand's taking me." My father, Frank, never liked parties.

"That should be fun," I say. Delores has taught me to play along, let her have her fantasies as long as they're not dangerous. "But you can finish the packing later. Delores and I are going to have some soup. She's made you a cup of tea and some of those oatmeal cookies you like, okay?"

She may not know who she is, or where she is, but she's in an agreeable mood tonight. She leaves the dress on the bed, closes the suitcase, and follows me into the kitchen. The cat, who's finished her visit to the litter box, follows her.

"What kind of dressing you want on your salad?" Delores asks me.

"Vinaigrette's fine, thanks. This soup smells wonderful."

"Would have been better with a ham bone, but I did it like you said."

"It's healthier this way."

"You got nothing to worry about, skinny as you are." She turns to my mother. "Watch out now, Miz Margaret. That tea's hot. And *you,*" she says to the cat, who's rubbing her back against Delores's thigh, "you go on over there, finish your dinner." She points to the bowl by the refrigerator. "At least this varmint's cleaner than that dog. Whatever happened with those people, anyway? They still together?"

"So far."

"Good," says Delores. "Once you been married long as they were, you might as well stick it out. She ever go to court for that burglary business? The Hart lady, I mean."

"The case was dismissed."

"Figures. Rich old lady like that, she can pay her way out of trouble. Couldn't make that stuff up! Two old people getting a divorce, fighting over their little dog! Crazy judge gives the dog a lawyer, like he's a human or something. Old woman says the old man's running around on her, but then it turns out *she's* the one out in the middle of the night, only not for what you think—no, she's out breaking into people's houses stealing their dogs!"

"She wasn't 'stealing,' she was rescuing the dogs from abusive owners."

"But she gets herself *arrested,*" Delores says, chuckling.

"It wasn't very funny at the time," I say.

"But then they get back together and the case is over, and when the news people show up at the old lady's door, she tells them all about how lawyer Sally Baynard is a miracle worker!"

"She might have been a little drunk."

"So you think they'll stay together now?" asks Delores.

"I'm no an expert on long-term relationships. You're the one who managed to stay in love for twenty years."

"But we weren't married until the very end."

"Maybe that's the reason," I say.

"It's not that simple," says Delores. "Use your napkin, Miz Margaret." Tea dribbles down my mother's chin.

"You always said you were better off not married."

"But it's not like there's one rule for everybody," she says. "You ain't me. I ain't you. Charlie and me, we worked it out to suit the two of us and we was mostly happy, but we could still have some wicked fights. . . . I don't mean hitting or anything . . . just words. We had one right before he died, 'cause he kept talking about how I needed to find somebody else when he was gone, and it made me mad."

"Well, he was right," I say.

"No," she says. "I can't get used to another man, 'specially not one who won't measure up to Charlie." Tears glisten in the corners of her eyes.

"There are a lot of good men out there, Delores."

"You should take your own advice sometimes."

After she leaves I help my mother with her shower, then into her nightgown. She doesn't object when I hang the green dress back in the closet. Just as she's falling to sleep she says, "I should have married Ed Shand."

I turn in early, glad for the comfort of my own bed, my quiet room, where for a few hours no one will need anything from me. Even Beatrice seems fine without much attention.

"It's weird," I tell Tony when he calls, "She's here in bed with me, but she's . . . I don't know exactly how to describe it . . . aloof. Maybe she's still getting used to me."

"Cats aren't like dogs," he says. "They're more reserved about showing affection."

"So it's not *me,* then."

"She's paying you a high compliment by just being near you at this point."

"She's purring."

"She's content," he says.

"We had a stressful afternoon." I tell him about the visit to the plantation, the conversation with Gail Sims. "I can't understand why Mrs. Mackay didn't just choose Gail. She and Beatrice are great together. She doesn't want to live in that big old house, but she and her fiancé have a place not far away, and they have cats of their own."

"That could be a problem."

"What do you mean?"

"Cats are territorial."

"She seemed to think it wouldn't be a problem."

"But didn't the old lady's will—"

"It's a trust."

"—didn't it say that the cat should live on the plantation?"

"Her son—Randall—wants the house. He'll get it anyway when the cat dies, but he wants it now. I can see his point. A cat doesn't need a plantation. And Randall won't object to Gail being paid to take care of Beatrice. It seems like such an obvious, practical solution."

"Except for the other cats."

"But Randall's threatening to challenge his mother's competency if I don't let Gail have the cat."

"Can he do that?"

"It's an uphill battle, and if he loses he could forfeit his remainder."

"His what?"

"What he gets after the cat dies. She put a special provision in the trust that says if he challenges it, and he loses, he forfeits that."

"Sounds like a pretty big chance for him to take."

"Which is why I think he's probably just threatening. But the last thing I want is to get tied up in litigation in the Probate Court."

"I thought you lawyers *like* litigation."

"But I'd be stuck with the cat while . . ." The moment I say this, Beatrice stops purring, as if she's insulted. "My life is complicated enough."

"What's so complicated?"

It aggravates me that he'd even ask this question, and maybe I'm a little sarcastic when I answer: "Well, let's see. There's my mother. My law practice. You."

"I'm a *complication?*"

"I just meant, I'm trying to take care of my mother, my clients, spend some time with you, and now I've got this cat to worry about."

"Sorry to add to your burdens."

"You know that's not what I'm saying. I'm looking forward to spending tomorrow night—"

"I thought you were going to stay the weekend."

"I'm taking my mother to church on Sunday morning—she likes to go, and she hasn't been in a while—so I should probably stay in town Saturday night. "

"I guess I'll take what I can get," he says.

"Okay if I bring the cat? She hates the car, but I don't want to leave her here with the sitter if I can help it."

"Sure. Bring the cat. Bring your mom. Bring your case files if you want to. What the hell."

"Unless you'd rather I not come at all."

He ignores this. "I'll have dinner ready. You got an old blanket?"

"I should bring my own bedding?"

It's a relief to hear him laugh. "For the cat. Cut up an old blanket, line the bottom of her carrier. She'll be more comfortable on the road. And bring a toy for her."

"I don't have any toys."

"Empty a pill container, put a few dried beans inside, screw the cap back on. She'll have a good time batting that around."

"See you tomorrow, then."

"I love you," he says.

"I love you, too," but I know how easy it is to say these words, and how difficult it is to live them.

Ladykiller

I often beat Gina to the office in the morning. Her A.M. routine is considerably more elaborate than mine. She needs an hour for her hair and makeup, she tells me, as if this daily ritual is a vital function. Though she's almost never more than a few minutes late, it irritates me when the elevator opens onto a dark office, especially this morning when I'm running late myself and I'm lugging the cat in her carrier, as well as the litter box, wrapped in a garbage bag. I'd like nothing more than to smell coffee already brewing.

Before I left home I gave Delores her Christmas bonus early, in hopes this might make her more amenable to cat-sitting, but she reminded me that she'd be taking my mother to the podiatrist, and I was nervous about her leaving Beatrice alone in the condo. "You act like that animal's your baby," Delores said. "Believe me, it don't care about you like you care about *it*! It'll be fine if you just put it in the bathroom, like the vet said, with some food and water."

"She's my responsibility until I can find her a home," I said. "I have a fiduciary duty to her."

"A what?"

"It means I have a legal and ethical responsibility to act in her best interests."

"People leave their cats alone all the time," she insisted.

"But I have a special relationship to Beatrice, just like I had a special relationship with Sherman."

"You can say that again! You and that little dog, you sure was a pair there for a while!"

"That's not what I mean. It has nothing to do with affection," I explained. "Because I have a special duty toward her, I have to take extra care that nothing bad happens to her."

"Don't mean you have to spend every waking minute with it. Good thing you never had children, they'd be spoiled rotten." She said this without thinking, while she wiped Mom's face after breakfast, but the words followed me out the door and all the way to the office. Whenever I lull myself into believing I'm okay with my childless life, someone will innocently utter a statement like this and send my mind wandering into a maze of what-might-have-beens, in search of the child who is always, when I imagine him, so much like my ex-husband Joe. Maybe that's why I've developed a reputation as an advocate for kids in Family Court—the abused and neglected, the ones at the center of vicious custody battles. Many of these mostly pro bono appointments have come from Joe; he knows I have a hard time saying no.

I turn on the lights in the hall, let Beatrice out, get the coffee going. She rubs her back against my ankles as if to say, "Thanks. I hate being hauled around in that thing."

"Oh, hi, you!" says Gina when she comes in, but not to me. The cat pauses long enough to acknowledge her entrance, then runs back to my office.

"Doughnuts?" I ask. "I thought you were on a diet."

"To celebrate!" she says, opening the box of Krispy Kremes, a dozen: glazed, chocolate covered and raspberry-filled. "Look!" She extends her left hand dramatically, her fingers caressing the air, so that I can't miss it: the diamond ring. "Isn't it gorgeous? I was totally surprised!"

"It's lovely."

"You don't sound very enthusiastic."

"It's from Rick?"

"Who else? I think it's a full carat."

I don't know anything about carats. "It really is beautiful," I say through the hole of a glazed doughnut.

"I know you think it's too soon."

"Gina, I'm not your mother." But then I can't help myself. "Rick's wife just died. He's hardly had time to—"

"But he was going to divorce her anyway. And he's a psychologist. He must know what he's doing."

"I hope you're right." I know Rick as well as any divorce lawyer knows her client, enough to know Gina's almost certainly wrong. Rick Silber may be an expert on personality disorders, but when it comes to understanding himself, he has about as much insight as a doughnut. "I'm really happy for you."

"Sometimes you just have to take a chance," she says, taking a bite of her doughnut, talking through the raspberry jelly. "I know we're way different, but it's not like there's a Mr. Perfect out there, you know."

"You really complement each other," I continue, doing the best I can. Gina is tall, beautiful, energetic, and upbeat. She had a baby right after high school, never went to college, split up with the dad after a couple of years, married again, divorced; but except in matters of romance she exhibits uncommon common sense. Rick is short, balding, and pudgy. Gina convinced him to buy a real pair of shoes to replace the sandals, and to shave the goatee, but her makeover did not extend to his neurotic self-absorption. He has a PhD in narcissism.

"Yes, I think so," she says, still admiring the ring.

"So, when's the wedding?"

"We haven't set a date. He wants to talk to you first."

"He needs my permission?"

"He just wants to talk to you. You know Rick. Sometimes he needs reassurance. Anyway, how did Beatrice do last night?"

"Okay. She slept with me half the night."

"Maybe you should keep her."

"I'm not on Mrs. Mackay's list. Speaking of which, would you make an appointment for that librarian to come in . . . what's her name . . . Katherine something . . . to come in next week?"

"Harleston," says Gina. "I already did. Monday morning."

"Would you mind watching Beatrice while I run over to Probate Court?"

"Sure, but I'm going over later, if you want me to pick up something."

"No, I need to talk to the judge."

"Don't forget the Vernelle deposition, here, at ten thirty."

"I should be back in plenty of time."

Judge Clarkson's desk is still covered with stacks of old files. When he stands to greet me he has to hold on to it to steady himself. "Too much history," he says, sighing. "I thought when I got elected probate judge I'd be escaping the frenzy of law practice, but every one of these"—he waves his hand over the files and the boxes cluttering the floor—"is a little drama. Sometimes a *big* drama with a lot of screaming and yelling. Even the ones that go smoothly can break your heart. Like this one." He picks up a thin file. "Widow had almost nothing. Paid her lawyer more money to draw up her will than her estate was worth. Mostly just a bunch of old furniture and costume jewelry, but she wanted to make sure each of her three daughters got some. Turned out she collected paperweights, and one of the damn things was worth a couple of thousand. Of course they fought over that one." He gestures for me to sit. "Normally I wouldn't be involved in such a small estate, but the deceased was a friend of a friend, so I helped them work it out. Anyway, I need to quit reminiscing if I'm ever going to close up shop and get out of here."

"Can't your secretary help you with these files?"

"Sure, she'd do a great job—put them all in order, send them out for storage—but then I wouldn't be able to say goodbye to them. You probably think I'm feeble-brained, but I spent my life with these people. But you didn't come in here to listen to an old man ramble. . . . What can I do for you?"

"I need your advice on the Mackay case." I tell him about my visit to Oak Bluff, the interview with Gail Sims, Randall Mackay's surprise appearance and his proposal. "I'm tempted to go along with it. Gail seems responsible, and the cat loves her. The only catch is that she doesn't want to live in the house. I know what the trust specifies, but it seems to me the most important thing is Beatrice's welfare, and if Gail is the right person, what difference does it really make whether she's living in a big house or a trailer?"

"Sounds like you've already made up your mind," he says.

"Not yet. That's why I wanted to talk to you. I've scheduled an interview with Katherine Harleston, the librarian, and I've made reservations to fly up to New York to see the other candidate, the nephew, but frankly it seems like a waste of time, and that I'd only be using up trust assets. And—Your Honor, with all due respect, when you asked me to take this case I didn't realize I was going to end up taking care of a cat."

"Let me ask you a question," he says. "Suppose a judge appointed you to represent a child whose parents had been killed in an automobile accident. They left no wills, no instructions as to who should be the child's guardian in the event of death. Three family members have come forward to say they'd be happy to take the child. You interview the first one, an aunt, say, and she seems nice enough, responsible, et cetera, et cetera, et cetera. Would you go to that judge and say, *I'm satisfied this one will do a good job, I don't need to investigate further.* Would you do that?"

"But sir, this is a cat, not a child."

He leans forward, locks his eyes on mine. "Apparently Lila Mackay felt closer to the cat than she did to her child. And just as a matter of principle, I wouldn't accept any 'deal' with Randall."

"But if he contests the trust, the cat could be in limbo for months . . . years, maybe."

"He has a year from the date of his mother's death to contest it, but he won't. He's a spoiled brat who never made anything of himself despite having all the advantages, but he's not stupid. Remember, if he challenges the trust and he loses, he forfeits what she left him. You know the law on testamentary capacity, I assume?"

"I've been reviewing it."

"He'd have the burden of proving incompetence at the time she signed the trust. Mind you, the legal test isn't that she must have had a reasonable basis for what she did, but that she had the capacity to *understand* what she did. Look at *Gaddy vs. Douglass*: 'Even an insane person may execute a will if it is done during a sane interval.' So once Randall consults a lawyer, he should come to his senses. Of course, I can't guarantee that. He might just be angry enough to . . . But look here," he says, "if you can't handle this, I'll find someone else. Probably plenty of starving young lawyers out there who'd be happy to take it on, black cat and all."

He hardly knows me, has no inkling of how the words "you can't handle this" bring back the Sally Baynard who'd stay up all night preparing for a trial, who would stand before the jury the next day making her opening argument, fighting exhaustion, fending off the judge who made a pass at her at lunchtime, battling a paternalistic prosecutor, dealing with the ungrateful and almost certainly guilty client. But when Sally Baynard took a bathroom break, she'd stand in the stall for an extra minute and silently repeat her mantra: *You can handle this.*

On the way back to the office I stop in Washington Park. It's a mild day, the air heavy with humidity. I need this five-minute respite, this brief anonymity. These tourists don't know me, hardly notice the middle-aged woman in the gray suit sitting on the bench under the giant live oak. The tour guide tells them about the earthquake of 1886, after which Charlestonians who'd lost their houses set up a tent city here. Some even brought their oriental rugs and silverware from home.

I try to imagine living in a tent with my mother. She would definitely insist on bringing her silverware. I'm lost in this thought when my cell phone rings.

"You still at the Probate Court?" asks Gina.

"Just left."

"Joe Baynard called. Said he needs to talk to you. I told him you had the deposition at ten thirty. He said it would just take a minute."

"What about?"

"He wouldn't say. For God's sake don't let him stick you with another bizarre pro bono . . . No, nothing much going on here except that Natalie Carter's husband—the judge—made an appointment for four thirty."

"I was going to try to leave a little early."

"He was pretty insistent. Said he wants to talk to you about the offer. He sounded kinda nice."

"That's a ruse."

"Anyway, I told him you could give him half an hour."

"How's Beatrice?"

"Fine. Curled up back there on your sofa, sleeping. She was playing with a big palmetto bug and that must have exhausted her."

"Yuck."

"She chased it around the office, caught it once and batted it around a little, then it got away. . . . You know how one minute those things are running around the floor and then all of a sudden they fly? It was a huge one. I've already called the exterminator."

My relationship with Joe is an ongoing drama for the Family Court set, the story line based loosely on fact but routinely spiced with fiction, which in the telling and retelling reinvents itself, acquiring new details, such as: (1) we split up because I wouldn't join the Junior League (true that Joe's mother wanted me to, but that had nothing to do with my leaving), and (2) that his father and uncle forced me out of the family firm (false). The drama experienced a revival during the dog case, with regular and sometimes contradictory broadcasts, such as: (3) I kept his name because I never fell out of love with him (false), and (4) I recently had sex with him at my condo, with my mother in the next room (false—it wasn't Joe, it was the vet).

And then there's: (5) I visit him in his chambers on a regular basis and we "do it" behind closed doors. False, of course. Though we've met in his office many times since our divorce, it's almost always with the door open. Yes, things did get messy during the dog case, but now that the case is over and Joe's back with Susan, I'm especially careful not to do or say anything he might misinterpret.

Which is why, when he motions for me to come in and close the door, I'm on guard.

"Thanks for coming," he says.

"I have a deposition at ten thirty."

"This won't take long. Relax—I'm not going to jump across the desk and grab you. This has nothing to do with you and me."

"Good!"

"You don't have to sound so relieved," he says. We're like two people fencing—lots of guarded dancing around each other, and then, when I least expect it, a lunge. "I had a strange call this morning," he continues. "from a guy I used to do some hunting with. Randall Mackay."

"He mentioned he knew you."

"I haven't seen him in years—which is why it's odd that he just calls me out of the blue, asks how I'm doing, lots of chitchat, then he finally gets around to the point, which is you."

"He's involved in one of my cases."

"The cat case."

"Right. But what was he calling *you* for?"

"Fishing."

"For what?"

"Feeling his way around, said he wanted my take on how you operate. I told him you're straightforward, honest. Tough but fair. I told him I hold you in the highest regard despite our divorce."

"Thanks."

"It happens to be true," Joe says. "But just after I said that, he says, 'Well, if you feel that way about her, you might want to tell her she'd be wise not to make this case any more difficult than it has to be.'"

"Don't worry, I've got it under control."

"You need to be careful around this guy, Sally."

"He's just angry because the cat's got his inheritance."

"He has a bad reputation. His first wife divorced him on physical cruelty. The second one disappeared."

"What do you mean, 'disappeared'?"

"The story was, he was teaching her how to shoot, they were doing target practice, she got hurt. Luckily the bullet just grazed her. She told everybody it was her fault, but a couple weeks later she left town and hasn't been heard from since."

"You think he shot her on purpose?"

"Word was, they'd both been drinking. She was some floozy who ran a roadhouse out on Edisto and he—at least he used to be—is a big boozer. Imagines himself quite the lady-killer."

"Well, I'm not going to fall for him, if that's what you're getting at."

"Okay, joke around if you want to. Just be careful."

"Warning accepted. Everything going okay with you?" This is a dangerous question.

He shrugs. "Livin' the dream: nice house, nice wife, kids in expensive prep schools, Yacht Club. And a great job, of course!" Some people might miss the hint of sarcasm in his voice, but I don't.

"You're frustrated in Family Court."

"You could say that."

"You still want a Circuit Court judgeship?"

"I'm thinking about it."

"If you want it, you'll get it. Your family can help you with the politicking."

"It's not as easy as it used to be." He's picking his nails. "*Nothing's* as easy as it used to be."

I almost ask him about his marriage, but catch myself. "Listen, I've got a deposition in ten minutes. Thanks for the heads-up on Randall Mackay."

"How's the dog?"

"It's a cat."

"No," he says, "I mean the little schnauzer. Sherman."

"He's fine. Never thought I'd miss him so much."

"Still got that photo of him on your desk?"

"Yeah. It's kind of silly, I guess."

"I don't remember you ever having a picture of *me* on your desk. . . . Never mind, scratch that." He follows me to the door. We shake hands. "Take care of yourself, Sally."

A Headache

———❦———

I'm stuck in late Friday afternoon traffic on my way to Tony's, the dull throb of a headache starting at the base of my skull, when I hear myself talking to the cat. She's on the seat beside me in her carrier, listening intently, as if there's absolutely nothing unusual about having a human unleash all her frustrations, beginning with the disastrous Vernelle deposition, at which my client, an anesthesiologist, complained that the temporary child support was "breaking" him, while later admitting that he'd just bought a new Maserati because he "got a great deal on it." The Maserati, of course, came as a surprise to me, despite our pre-deposition conference last week, during which we'd updated his financial declaration.

And Beatrice endures an even louder rant, this one about my meeting with Derwood Carter, Natalie's husband—*Who does he think he is, talking to me like that?*

I'd been prepared for his usual arrogance, his condescension, but I was naive to believe he might be coming to talk about compromise. Sure, he'd begun the conversation cordially enough, thanking me for this last-minute appointment, then taking my counterproposal from his coat pocket, unfolding it, and adjusting his reading glasses as if he meant to take it seriously. Then he'd said, his voice deliberately flat, devoid of emotion: "I just wanted to read this again before I throw it in that wastebasket." He "read" my letter in three seconds, then wadded it into a ball and lobbed it over my head into the metal can in the corner behind my desk. I didn't turn to look, but I knew he'd dunked it straight in.

"I used to play center on the high school team," he said. "Some skills you don't lose."

"Do you want to play basketball, or settle this case?" I asked, trying to keep my cool. "Because I'm not interested in basketball unless it's pro."

"Another skill I haven't lost," he said, "is knowing my women."

"Your 'women'? I guess that includes your court reporter." The one who travels with him when he holds court away from Beaufort, whose hotel room almost always has a door that opens into his.

"I was referring to Natalie, of course. And you. I know how Natalie operates, and it's clear she isn't going to tell you about her tryst with my old law partner. And I know how *you* think, so I'm assuming you believe her heavily edited story about our marriage. I thought I'd help you out with the facts before we begin any serious discussion about the terms of the settlement."

He then proceeded to read me the confession of his former law partner, an alcoholic completing the 12-step program. "You know they're supposed to apologize to everyone they've hurt, right?" This well-meaning fellow's letter to Derwood, dated two months ago, was tastefully brief but to the point: *Fifteen years ago, when I told you our affair was over, that was true. But recently I succumbed to temptation again. I take full responsibility for this. As I trust Natalie has already told you, she is as ashamed as I am. It will not happen again. I hope that you will find it in your heart to forgive me.*

Before Derwood left he said, "When your client has given you an accurate rendition of the facts, I'll be happy to entertain a more real-istic settlement offer."

Now as I cross the Wappoo Cut and turn onto Maybank High-way, the heavy traffic is behind me, but I can't get his smile out of my head. "I hate him!" I shout. Beatrice jumps. "Sorry," I say, and she settles again. The throb at the base of my skull builds into a full-blown headache. The cat, however, seems perfectly content. Maybe she likes nestling in the old towel the vet recommended.

By the time we turn onto the dirt road leading to Tony's house, it's already dark. I brake for a buck who appears out of nowhere, jumps a fence, and disappears into the night. Farther on, where the road winds through the marsh, I slow for a porcupine lumbering along, its quills lit by the headlights, until it, too, disappears.

Tony's left the porch light on. "We're almost there," I tell Be-atrice. Though I can't see it, I can feel the open space around us, the acres of lowlands, marsh, and creek, and the pressure in my head eases a little. We're less than twenty miles from the city but already Charleston seems like another world: my mother, my ex-husband, my office, the courthouse, the cases. Even Derwood Carter's satisfied smile recedes into the darkness.

Tony opens the door for us, relieves me of the carrier and puts it on the kitchen counter. All the dogs crowd around, their three noses pointed up. "Relax, sweetie," Tony says.

"I have a headache," I respond.

"I was talking to the cat," he says. "But to you, too . . ." He gives me a kiss, pours me a glass of wine. "Hungry? I made some vegetarian chili." He's not much of a cook, but he's mastered the Crock-Pot.

"That sounds great." He's set the table: mismatched utensils, frayed place mats curled at the edges from years of washing, candles in wooden candlesticks that are coated with layers of old candle wax.

He serves the chili, lights the candles, turns off the overhead light. "There," he says. "That should help." The cat settles in her carrier on the counter, and the dogs vie for the space under the table. I can feel a warm head settle across my feet. "Now, tell me about your day. Unless it will make the headache worse."

I tell him about Gina's announcement, the conference with Judge Clarkson, the deposition, the late afternoon meeting with my client's husband, doing my best to preserve confidentiality, but I slip up on "damn Derwood Carter." Fortunately the name means nothing to him. He listens, nods, waits until I'm finished to speak: "That's a lot for one day, but I'm sure you've dealt with worse."

"I'm getting too old for this."

"Oh, come on."

"I mean it." I won't tell him about my conversation with Joe.

"Well, let's take it one problem at a time," he says. "The Gina thing—she's a big girl, she can handle her own love life, don't you think?"

"She hasn't done a very good job so far."

"Did she ask you for advice?"

"Not really, but she's more than just my secretary. She's a friend."

"So if it works out, you'll be happy for her. If it doesn't, you'll be there for her. In the meantime she's only going to resent you if you try to change her mind."

"I'm not even sure she *should* change her mind."

"Now, about the woman who's screwing her husband's law partner—"

"*Ex*-law partner, but that's irrelevant."

"She's not the first client who's ever lied to you, is she?"

"Of course not. But I felt like a fool, having to find it out from her husband. You don't know this guy. It was humiliating. I'm going to lose the case."

"Remember what you told me once?" he says, smiling. "Something about chicken poop?"

"You can't make chicken salad out of chicken poop."

"That's it. This lady—your client—*she* screwed things up, not you. Then she lied to you. So if you can't make chicken salad out of her chicken poop, it's not your fault. But knowing you, you've got some pretty good recipes for chicken poop."

He knows how to make me laugh. "Maybe I'll have another glass of wine."

"Want some leftover apple pie?" he asks.

"No thanks. The chili was great."

"Relax while I clean up."

"I can clean up."

"Not when you have a headache," he says. He peers into the cat carrier. "She seems pretty laid back."

"I need to feed her."

"I'll do it. Come on, sweetie." He lifts Beatrice out. "The dogs won't hurt you. They're just curious. Suzie and Sheba . . . Carmen . . . go visit with Sally." He points, and after a parting sniff around Beatrice, the dogs join me in the living room, the beagle next to me on the sofa, the retrievers near my feet.

"So," he says, "that old probate judge won't let you off the hook, will he?"

"He made me feel guilty. But I'm in a bind. I don't want to leave Beatrice at the condo—Delores has enough on her hands, just dealing with Mom. And it's a hassle to haul her back and forth to the office every day."

"I guess I could help you out for a while."

"You'd take her?" The cat looks up from her bowl of food.

"She'd be okay here for a week or two until you finish the case."

"It shouldn't take that long. Technically, I shouldn't, but—"

"'Technically,' that old judge should be stuck with the cat—at least until he chooses a caregiver, right?'"

"True, but he's assigned that duty to me, and I guess I've accepted. I can't just give her away, even temporarily."

"Nobody expects you to be with the cat twenty-four hours a day. She'll be living with you, but during the days you're at work, she'll be here. I usually come home for lunch; I can check on her."

"How can she live with me if she's here?"

"Because," he says, "you'll be living here, too."

"Oh, I see." The beagle hears the strain in my voice, lifts her head off my lap, relaxes again when I stroke the back of her head. "But I can't do that."

"Of course you can. You said the sitters are working out okay."

"They are, but it isn't twenty-four/seven care. Delores comes on weekdays, and Shenille only fills in at night if I need her."

"Maybe she'd be willing to work more. Or you could hire another one. Didn't you have a third person?"

"Mom didn't like her. I don't want to upset her." I feel the headache coming back. "And this feels like you're bribing me—"

"'Bribing' you?"

"You'll take the cat, but only if I agree to move in with you."

"Look," he says, standing up, looking down at me, "I'm trying to help you solve your problem. You don't want to leave Beatrice at your condo while you're at work—"

"It's not fair to Delores."

"And you don't want to haul her back and forth to your office every day."

"Not really."

"So, I'm offering to keep her here. And you don't have to feel guilty about abandoning her, because you'll be here at night."

"But I'll be abandoning my mother."

"Okay, so you don't spend *every* night here. Stay in town a couple of nights a week, whatever."

"I'll consider it."

"That sounds like a lawyer talking."

"You're pressuring me," I say.

He starts toward the bedroom, then turns back toward me: "You're right. Forget it." I've never heard his voice like this. "I shouldn't have to negotiate my way into your heart." He stomps into the bedroom, comes back with a pillow and a comforter. "You might as well sleep out here. Wouldn't want you to feel any pressure."

The dogs follow him. He closes the door—not exactly a slam, but a statement nevertheless—and I'm left with Beatrice, whose pressure, as she curls against my chest, is both a reassurance and a worry.

Just a Little Trip

———◆———

The wind rattles the window behind the sofa and the full moon glares in at me like a disapproving father. When I pull the comforter over my head I dislodge Beatrice, who jumps to the floor. She stares at me coolly—*So, you're going to abandon me, too?*—and not until her eyes close can I fall back to sleep.

Sometime before dawn I feel her tongue like sandpaper raking my cheek and I push her away, too hard. "Sorry," I whisper, and she's right back, insistent, meowing. I sit up. The clothes I've slept in feel clammy. "Okay, calm down." She swipes the front door with her paw, and when this doesn't elicit the desired response from me, she swipes it again. "No, Beatrice, you've got your litter box in the kitchen, remember?" It's only then that I hear the hum of the motor, see the dim shape of the car through the window—no headlights— disappearing down the dirt road.

I coax Beatrice into my arms and then into her carrier. I'm about to leave when I feel a hand on my shoulder. There's a split second of terror before I realize it's Tony. "Did you hear that?" he asks.

"Someone must have made a wrong turn," I say.

"Long way to come down this road for a wrong turn." He turns on the overhead light. "I'm sorry about last night. I should have given you the bed." He takes the cat carrier from me. "Stay for some coffee, at least, so we can talk about it."

"I'm not going to change my mind."

"I shouldn't have made my offer to keep the cat conditional on your moving in."

"No, you shouldn't have. But I don't blame you for being frustrated."

"I just thought, since you spend some nights here anyway, a few more wouldn't be that big a deal for you. I don't know what's going on in your head, why what seems to me like the easiest, most natural thing is so problematic for you."

"It's not easy, with my mother."

"Let's pretend—and I know this sounds insensitive, but I don't mean it to be—that your mother's no longer in the picture. If she died tomorrow, would you want to be with me—all the time?" We're face-to-face, his hands on my shoulders.

"I—I guess so."

"You 'guess' so?"

"That's not really a fair question."

His hands drop to his side. "I think it *is*." He clears his throat, lowers his voice, but I can hear the anger. "Because if you're just using your mother as an excuse to postpone a decision about *us*, that's not okay with me. I've told you I'm willing for her to live with us. I've told you I'm willing to move closer to town, or to have her out here. I'm being as flexible as I know how to be, but it's never enough."

"You've been wonderful, Tony."

"So think about it. That question."

"Okay."

"Now what about the coffee?"

"I should get going." I reach for the carrier, but he holds on to it.

"I'll help you out with Beatrice for the time being. "He shrugs and smiles. "I guess as long as she's here, I can pretend you're here, too." He kisses me, a kiss that—is it my imagination?—seems guarded, abbreviated.

"You sure?"

"If there's anything I can handle, it's an animal. Women are another story."

As I drive away, my relief is shadowed by a feeling I can't name, not quite guilt or shame but an uneasiness at my core. Is it about leaving the cat, or the vet?

Where the road crosses the creek the rising sun shines in my face, highlighting the dirty windshield, and it's only when I turn on the washer that I notice the piece of paper, the wiper having carried it across the glass. I stop to retrieve it. It's wet, the ink running, but I can make out the words: *Dear Miss Trust Enforcer, your investigation brings you to the most interesting places. Don't kill yourself looking for the solution that's right under your nose.*

It's not signed.

I stop at the Harris Teeter for groceries. It's still early, so there aren't many other shoppers. I'm usually efficient, disciplined, but today I linger at the deli counter sampling the cheeses, then choose a Camembert and my mother's favorite Swiss. Nearby a guy in a chef's hat stirs a skillet of chicken and snow peas, offers me a sample in a little paper cup with a doll-sized plastic spoon. "No thanks, not today," I say, then give in. I haven't eaten chicken in years, but I'm hungry.

"Nice, huh?" he says. "The secret's a half-cup of white wine near the end, when you put the snow peas in. They shouldn't cook longer than a minute or so. . . . Ms. Baynard?"

"Donnie?"

He grins. "Been a while, hasn't it? I hear you left the public defender."

I can't remember his last name, vaguely connect this face to a younger one, a skinny kid who stood next to me in the courtroom, trembling before the judge handed down the sentence. "I have my own practice, on Broad Street. And you—how long have you been doing this?"

"Just got the gig. Want some more?"

"No, thanks, but it's delicious."

"Yeah, I'm learning how to cook. Thinking maybe I can get into that cooking school at Tech, once I save up some money."

He hands me the recipe, printed on a card. "Thanks," I say. "I'll try it."

"You saved my life, you know that?" He pushes the chef's hat up a little, wipes his forehead with the back of his hand, readjusts the hat, and now I remember that gesture. Back then it was a baseball cap. *Leave the cap at home when you come to court*, I'd advised. *Can you borrow a suit?* He said he'd try. And when he showed up for his guilty plea—receiving stolen goods—the sleeves of his suit jacket hung almost to his fingertips.

"It was a miracle you got me probation," he says now. "Even my own mom said I didn't deserve it. Anyway, I don't want to keep you."

"Nice seeing you again, Donnie. You take care."

"You have a blessed day, Ms. Baynard."

Maybe I didn't save Donnie, as he believes I did, but I remember now how hard I worked to keep him out of jail. He claimed he didn't know that the two brand-new TV sets, still in their boxes, were stolen goods. "Don't you believe me?" he asked. It didn't matter. No jury, I explained, would believe his story. After wrangling a recommendation of probation out of the assistant solicitor, I convinced

Donnie to plead. There was no guarantee the judge would accept the recommendation, of course—and if he didn't, Donnie was exposing himself to a possible five years in prison—but it was likely. On the morning of the plea I assembled an impressive cast of characters to vouch for him: his mother, his grandmother, an elderly aunt, his junior high football coach, his minister, a neighborhood shopkeeper who promised him a job. The judge gave him probation, but what I remember most about that day was the look on Donnie's face as each of these people spoke in turn. When it was over he wept—this tough kid from the projects—and said to me, "I never knew all those good things about myself."

The Sally Baynard who got probation for Donnie all those years ago wasn't any miracle worker, but she was determined, dedicated, energized by even the most hopeless case. That Sally wouldn't be unnerved by a note on the windshield.

That Sally would fight for the cat.

"Your mama's still asleep," says Shenille when I get home.

"How was she last night?"

"Didn't want to go to bed at her usual time, so I just let her sit up watching TV with me until she started to nod off. We get along just fine, your mama and me. She's so sweet." My mother is many things, but she isn't sweet. These days she can be a holy terror. But Shenille's new at the job. She's trying to reassure me, and probably herself.

"You want me to help you put those groceries away?" she says. "I got nowhere I have to be right now. Kennie's doing double shift at the shipyard."

"No, thanks, you go on."

But she hangs around another half hour, telling me about a "friend" whose husband has been abusing her. "He never hits her in the face, just bruises her in places you can't see." I explain how to go about getting a restraining order, how much abuse is necessary for a divorce on the ground of physical cruelty. She shakes her head. "No, she doesn't believe in divorce. I think maybe things might go better between them if she quit her job. He doesn't like it that his wife works."

"Does she know about My Sister's House—the women's shelter?"

"Yes, ma'am."

"You give her my phone number, if she wants to talk about it."

"She can't afford a downtown lawyer."

"Tell her not to worry. We can work it out."

"That's mighty nice of you."

I've had conversations like this many times. There's no "friend." There's only Shenille, afraid, hoping that somehow her problem will go away.

Mom doesn't wake up until almost eleven. I make her favorite breakfast—scrambled eggs and bacon and a slice of toast with orange marmalade—but she eats only two bites of egg and one of the bacon strips. She won't touch the toast. "It's the wrong color!" she yells.

"It's the same as always," I say.

"I want it red!"

"You don't like strawberry, Mom."

"I want it red!"

"I don't think we have any, Mom."

"I have my red dress for the trip."

"We aren't going anywhere today. Here, why don't you try . . ." But I can't convince her to eat more, can't distract her. "Okay, I tell you what. It's a nice day. Why don't you and I take a little trip?" Now her face relaxes. "But you have to get dressed first."

It takes almost an hour for me to help her shower, get dressed. She wants to wear the red dress, the one she's laid out on the bed. "I've got my suitcase ready to go!" she says. The suitcase lies open on the easy chair, ready for the journey to who-knows-where. Only when I agree that we can take it with us can I cajole her into slacks and a sweater.

"Oh," says Mrs. Furley in the elevator as we ride down. "You're going on vacation?"

"Just a little trip," I explain.

"Yes," my mother adds, "We're going to a party."

"How nice," says Mrs. Furley.

"And I'm getting married," says Mom, smiling. "I married the wrong man the first time."

Mrs. Furley gives me an *Oh, I see* look. "Well, I'm sure you'll be very happy," she says.

If I take the direct route to the Battery, down East Bay Street, our "trip" would be only about a mile, so I cheat, drive west on Calhoun and over the causeway toward Folly Beach, then turn around and head back to town, crossing the Ashley River again. I take Broad Street over to Meeting and down to the tip of the peninsula, driving slow enough for her to savor this other world of historic mansions and formal gardens behind ornate wrought iron gates. She's calmer now, as if she's where she wants to be.

All her life she's imagined herself the kind of woman who would live in one of these houses, told me stories about "our lost plantation," our "lost fortune." She'd say, "We're from a very old family," as if everyone alive wasn't. I was in my thirties before I discovered, from a cousin, that the family "plantation" was only a few hardscrabble acres in Alabama, sold long ago because my ancestor had run out of "old money." And there was never a mansion, nothing like the huge white-columned house we park in front of, a block from the Battery.

"What a lovely town!" she exclaims.

"Let's take a walk, and then we'll get a nice lunch somewhere." I hold on to her, which she resists, but I can't risk her falling. Getting her across the street into the park is an ordeal—she stops halfway and says she's forgotten her purse. "It's back at the condo, Mom." Thank God she doesn't remember the suitcase in the trunk. By the time we've walked around White Point Gardens she's worn out. I'm searching for an empty bench when the little dog runs up to me. "Look, Mom, it's Sherman!"

He dances around us, barking that sharp staccato bark that means he's discovered something special. When I bend down to pick him up, his delight propels him right into my arms. I've missed the smell of him, his wet nose nuzzling my neck. Following close behind is Rusty Hart, breathless: "I just let him off the leash for a minute!" Mr. Hart hasn't lost any weight but looks much better than when I last saw him, after his heart attack. "Calm down, buddy," he says to Sherman.

"Mr. Hart, I don't think you've met my mother, Margaret. Mom, this is Rusty Hart."

Mom stands a little straighter, pushes her hair up and away from her face as if she's a model posing for a photographer. "We're going to a party," she says.

"Well, don't let me keep you," says Mr. Hart. "Sherman and I were just occupying ourselves while Maryann deals with the real estate lady. She finally came to her senses about that money pit!" He points toward his house on East Bay Street.

"You're selling it?"

"Listing it soon. But the agent says we need to 'stage' it first— whatever that means—for the open house."

"Open house!" says my mother. "We'd be delighted!"

"Not now, Mom."

Her face falls. Mr. Hart and I exchange looks. "Why don't you come by the house for a minute," he says, "and say hello to Maryann?"

"Thank you," says my mother as Rusty Hart opens the front door for her, and to me she whispers, "Such a gentleman!" Inside she stands in the entrance hall and stares up at the chandelier, its crystals catching the light. "My grandmother had one just like it!" she says. This is the kind of home she always wanted: grand, historic, perfectly renovated. How many times did she tell me that our brick bungalow in Columbia was "just temporary, until we can find something nicer"?

"We can't stay," I say to Maryann. "I know you're busy."

"The agent just left," Maryann says. "Do sit down. . . . I'll make some coffee." Mrs. Hart is exquisitely dressed, as usual: teal green cashmere sweater, matching slacks, silver bracelet and earrings.

"No, really, we—" I protest, but my mother has already made herself at home.

"It's 'Margaret,' isn't it?" says Mrs. Hart to my mother. "You must be very proud to have such an accomplished daughter."

"She's a slut!"

"Mom, please—" I start, but Mrs. Hart, a woman accustomed to smiling her way through the most difficult social situations, hardly hesitates: "Well, I hope you won't mind our mess—we're rearranging things for the sale." Sherman hops up on the sofa next to her, nestles his head in her lap. "Did Rusty keep you on your leash, darling?"

Mr. Hart shoots me a look. "Wouldn't want to have *too* much fun, would we?"

"So," I say, "you'll be living at the beach full-time now?"

"Yes," Maryann says. "Rusty says we can't afford to keep both houses. Of course, I would prefer to stay here, but he—"

"Why don't you just divorce me," says Mr. Hart, "marry the Prince of Wales, and keep this one?"

"I talked to your secretary the other day," continues Maryann. "She said you were busy with a new cat."

"I'm just keeping her temporarily."

"Oh, that's a shame. A pet would be such a comfort for you, since you have no children."

"We're taking a little trip," says my mother.

"Oh, how nice!" says Mrs. Hart brightly. "If Rusty weren't such a homebody, we'd get away more often. First, it was 'I'm working too hard,' and now that he's retired, it's . . .'"

They're still carping when we leave. I'd thought Mom hadn't noticed, but in the car she says, "That's the way your father and I were. Miserable."

"I don't remember it being all that bad."

"You weren't married to him."

"What about something special for lunch, Mom? Magnolias, maybe?"

"That poor little dog, listening to that all the time."

"I think he's what keeps them together."

"We should get a dog."

"Maybe we will, Mom, but first I need to find a good home for the cat. And remember, Delores doesn't like dogs."

"Delores liked Sherman. She just wouldn't admit it." Sometimes my mother is unusually perceptive. "Do you think he remembered me?" she asks, her voice again childlike. "Sherman?"

"Sherman? Sure he did."

"Ed Shand used to say I was unforgettable." She flips the visor down, checks her lipstick in the mirror. "I should have married him."

The Powers of Darkness

———◆———

Katherine Harleston, the librarian, arrives at my office half an hour early. "I hope you don't mind that I asked my husband to come along," she says. They're fortyish, she in a prim brown suit with a skirt that covers her knees, he in the standard Charleston good-old-boy costume—navy blazer, khaki slacks, tasseled loafers buffed to a high shine. She's square-jawed, thin-lipped, pale.

"That's fine," I say, but before I've even finished explaining my role in the case, he interrupts.

"We understand the terms of the trust, Ms. Baynard. I hope you won't think me presumptuous, but I can save you a lot of trouble. Katherine and I—"

"Hugh," she says, "You promised. . . ."

"I'm just trying to expedite things," he says.

"Why don't you tell me a little bit about yourself," I say, addressing my question to Katherine.

"Hugh and I have been married for nineteen years," she begins.

"Quite happily," he says.

"We have no children."

"How did you come to know Mrs. Mackay?" I ask Katherine.

"She and I developed a friendship when she came to the library to do research," she says. "That was about a year after I started working there, in the mid-nineties. She would come into town once or twice a week and I'd help her with her projects."

"What kind of projects?"

"She wrote articles for local and regional magazines, mostly about the history of Edisto . . . the plantations, the families. Before her heart attack she was planning to work on the history of the African-American churches out there. Lila was so energetic . . . it's a shame she never got her PhD. I admired her so much—" She stops, swallows. "I'm sorry. I miss her so—"

"You forgot to mention," her husband interrupts again, "that after she stopped driving to town, you would visit her regularly. You were almost like a daughter to her."

"Hugh exaggerates, but we were close," says Katherine. "Lila always encouraged me in my own work. And she was so . . . so *wise*. After Ricky—our son—died—"

"We don't need to go into that," Hugh says.

"After our son died—this was about five years ago—I had a very difficult time. Lila was like a mother to me. She encouraged me to apply for the head librarian job. I didn't get it, but just knowing she had such faith in me helped a great deal."

"Tell me about your relationship with Beatrice," I say.

"Katherine's always been a cat lover," Hugh says.

She smiles. "I've adopted some over the years, but we lost the last one about a month ago. Onyx. We called her Nix for short. Nix and Beatrice were sisters."

"Really?"

"Yes. About seven ago I went to the shelter, looking for a cat, and there were these two darling black kittens, almost identical. I brought them both home but Hugh said I could keep only one, so

I asked Lila, who'd just lost her cat. . . . It was hard to tell Onyx and Beatrice apart! Lila adored Beatrice. The bond between them was truly remarkable. Did you know that she used to read stories to—"

"She doesn't need to hear all this, Katherine," Hugh says.

I'd like to slap him. "Actually, the pet trust specifies that the chosen caretaker should provide, to the extent possible, the same emotional environment Mrs. Mackay would have provided for Beatrice, so the more I know about Mrs. Mackay, the easier my task will be."

"Well, I certainly wouldn't ever be able to *replace* Lila," says Katherine, "but I think I understand why her relationship with Beatrice was so special, because I feel the same way about cats. I don't consider them to be inferior creatures—just different from us. As a matter of fact, before Lila got so sick, we were working on a grant application . . . to bring Peter Singer to the library for a symposium."

"The animal rights expert?"

"Some people consider him rather extreme in his views, but Lila and I . . . Anyway, she treated Beatrice with the utmost respect, as a fellow creature. She was affectionate, but she was also very firm when she needed to be. She taught Beatrice to respect her in return. They really had a wonderful relationship. I feel so sorry for the cat now, without her."

"So," I continue, "I take it that you'd be willing to move out to the island, because as you know, the trust specifies—"

"Of course," says her husband. "We'd be delighted to do that."

"But wouldn't it be a long commute for you?" I ask Katherine.

"Well, if you were to choose me . . . I mean *us*," she says, "I would probably retire from the library. Hugh has his own business, which he can really operate from anywhere."

"What do you do?" I ask him.

"I have a high-end antiques business, mostly English furniture, antique garden statuary. I serve a very select group of customers."

"So you'd be using the house as a store?"

"Oh, no. I don't need a physical location," he says. "I take two or three buying trips each year, ship the items directly to the customers. But I do think I could help with the restoration of the Mackay property and furnishings."

Katherine shrugs. "Lila had a hard time keeping things up, especially in her later years. It wasn't the money, she just wasn't interested in—how should I say it?—material things."

"Oak Bluff could be a real showplace," Hugh says.

"But of course that has nothing to do with Beatrice," says Katherine.

"You understand," I explain, "that whomever I choose will only live in the house as long as the cat's alive?"

"Of course," Hugh says.

"And the income from the investments can be used only for the caretaker's salary—fifty thousand dollars—and for Beatrice's veterinary expenses, and of course for the maintenance of the house and property."

"Yes," Hugh says. "Don't worry, Katherine and I wouldn't be doing this for the money."

"But I need to be honest," Katherine says. "My job at the library is officially only part-time. I end up working almost full-time to get the job done. I'd love to have the time for my own work."

"Katherine is writing a historical novel," Hugh explains.

"Yes," she continues, "Lila always said a woman needed a room of her own, and money of her own."

"Do you know Gail Sims, the young woman who's been doing the maintenance and the groundskeeping?" I ask.

"I met her a couple of times, when she came out to cut the grass," she says. "She's nice enough, but—"

"She isn't the kind of person who belongs in that house," says Hugh.

"She's a sweet girl," says Katherine, "but . . . I don't know how to say this nicely . . . she's comes from a rather modest background. Of course, I won't deny that she loves Beatrice, and vice versa."

"A cat will love anybody who feeds it," says Hugh.

Katherine leans forward. "But you must understand that Beatrice is special. She's highly intelligent, sensitive and intuitive. She'll know if she's with the wrong person. I've often wondered if she's not a mind-reader!"

"My wife has a big imagination," says Hugh.

"What I mean is, I think she knew that Lila was her soul mate, not just her caregiver."

"Did Mrs. Mackay have other friends?" I ask.

"She didn't get into Charleston much in the last years," says Katherine. "She lived so far out of town, not many of her Charleston friends kept up with her. It was sad."

"What about someone named Simon?"

"That doesn't ring a bell," she says. "But I didn't know many of her set. They were so much older."

Just before they leave, Katherine asks me, "Where's Beatrice now?"

"She's living with me. But I'm hoping to finish my investigation soon."

"Let us know if you have any other questions," says Hugh.

"One more—can you think of any reason Mrs. Mackay didn't include *your* name along with your wife's?"

Katherine shoots a look at him, hesitates before she says: "We were separated briefly, about the time she set up the trust."

. . .

Ellen and I meet at our usual lunch spot, Poogan's Porch. She looks terrible. She's been my friend since law school, so I know that anxious smile. I remember it from those last couple of days before the bar exam, and I've seen it in the courtroom, when things aren't going well for her in trial.

"I've already ordered for you," she says. "Salmon spinach salad, without the salmon, right?"

"You in a hurry?"

"I have a staff meeting at one thirty."

"Everything okay?"

"Not exactly." *Oh God,* I think, *please tell me Ellen and Hank aren't splitting up.* The term "perfect couple" may be an oxymoron, but they're as close to perfect as any couple I know. "I had a horrendous weekend. I—just—" She can't catch her breath.

I reach across the table, touch the top of her hand. "Whatever it is, we'll deal with it." And then the other horrible possibilities race through my brain. Her mother died young of metastatic breast cancer.

She inhales as if it's going to be her last breath. "Mandy's pregnant."

Mandy is her daughter, her only child, a senior in high school, an A student and soccer star. "How far along?"

"A couple of months. You know how I've always told her to come to me when she had a problem? Well, she listened about the 'problem' part, but she must not have been paying attention to my speech about birth control."

"Who's the father?"

"Peter Matthews. You probably know his parents from Grace Church—Helen and John. I could kill them."

"Are they being obnoxious about it?"

"No, I mean Mandy and Peter. I lost it with Mandy."

"Well, I guess you're entitled," I say.

"I feel like my life's coming apart."

"If there's anyone I know who can handle a crisis, it's you."

"Mandy wants to keep it," says Ellen.

I absorb this while the waiter brings our meals and refills our iced tea, hovering too long, asking if we have everything we need, if we're enjoying this pleasant weather, if we're tourists. He's new here, just trying to do a good job, but the absence of our usual waitress seems like one more sign that things are coming apart. "She may change her mind."

"You know how strong-minded she is. When she decides she wants something, she won't let go. I told her, *Honey, this is different. This isn't the state soccer championship or the SAT—this is a baby. You'd be throwing your whole life away.* She got early admission to Duke, and on full scholarship. What's she going to do, go up to Durham with a *baby*? She says if she has to, she'll postpone college for a couple of years, get a job."

"Well, I know that's not what you want for her, but it's not impossible." I'm doing my best to sound steady, but I'm thinking, *This is a nightmare.*

"Would you talk to her? She respects you."

"Of course I will."

"I'm at the end of my rope."

"How's Hank dealing with it?"

"He's been having some problems at work, so I haven't told him yet." Hank's a lawyer with a big firm downtown. "This isn't public yet, but his firm's being gobbled up by Morfum and Chandler."

The name is vaguely familiar. "They're opening an office in Charleston?"

She nods. "It's a huge firm. Atlanta, New York, Dallas, Chicago."

"So, I guess that's not all bad."

"Except they're going to be conducting what they call an 'efficiency review,' and it seems that Hank may be superfluous."

"But he's got a great reputation. He'll find another—"

"Maybe, but I feel like . . . like everything we've worked so hard for . . . like it's all dissolving."

"Let's take this one step at a time," I say. "Has Mandy seen a doctor?"

"She has an appointment with Cheryl Feingold, next week."

"Cheryl's good."

"I know, but she's in our book group, so it's going to be all over town."

"Ellen." I lean over the table, look her in the eyes. "Cheryl won't blab, but if Mandy keeps the baby, sooner or later everyone will know. That's the least of your problems. The people who love you will support you, and the rest of them . . . who gives a damn *what* they think?"

"You're right, but it's hard. She needs to go to college."

"She will."

"With a baby?"

"You'd have to help her."

"She won't even consider adoption," says Ellen. "That's why I want you to talk to her."

"Of course I will. Now eat your lunch."

She smiles. "I love you."

"I love you, too."

"So," she says, taking a bite of her salad. "Enough about me. What's going on with you?"

"Nothing new." I won't burden her with my troubles today. I realize how lopsided our friendship has become: I unload on her, she settles me down. Hardly ever, lately, does it go the other way.

"What's going on with the cat case?" she asks.

"Tony's keeping the cat for a while," I say, my voice in neutral. "By the way, do you know Katherine Harleston? She works at the county library." Ellen knows everybody in Charleston.

"She's in the Junior League with me. Nice enough. We've been on a couple of committees together. She always follows through."

"What about her husband?"

"He's got some kind of antiques business, but I don't think he makes much." Ellen leans toward me. "I probably shouldn't tell you this, and it wasn't my case, but . . . a couple of years ago he was on the verge of being indicted for insurance fraud. . . . I heard he intimidated the assistant solicitor who was handling it."

"Who was that?"

"I can't remember." She looks at her watch. "Got to go." She hugs me. "You made me feel a lot better."

"I didn't fix anything."

"But you didn't feed me platitudes, like my sister: *It's a blessing in disguise. . . . God works in mysterious ways,* and all that."

I should work on the brief due next week, but when I close the door to my conference room, there's the Beatrice Box. I find the stack of letters from "Simon."

Dear Lila,

Thanks for your last note. No, I don't believe in ghosts—at least, not the otherworldly kind. But I am certain we can be haunted by our own pasts, our mistakes and our regrets. Perhaps the "presence" you sometimes feel so strongly is something like that? He's friendly, but ceaseless in his roaming through that old house of yours, looking for his lost love.

I may ramble a bit here, but do you remember Christopher Smart's poem Jubilate Agno? *As you know, I'm not a religious man, but think there's something divine about cats, and this poem captures (poor metaphor, perhaps) that divinity. Smart had the bad fortune to be thrown into prison for "lunacy"—this was in the mid-1700s, if I recall correctly—but the good fortune to have his cat as his companion. It's a long poem. When you next come to town I'll lend you my anthology, but here are just a few (divine) lines:*

> *For I will consider my Cat Jeoffrey.*
> *For he is the servant of the Living God duly and daily serving him. . . .*
> *For when his day's work is done his business more properly begins.*
> *For he keeps the Lord's watch in the night against the adversary.*
> *For he counteracts the powers of darkness by his electrical skin*
> *and glaring eyes. . . .*

My dear, we both know about the "powers of darkness," don't we? The devil manifests himself in many forms. Not just evil, but that wily demon, depression. I hope that Beatrice will help you against that old adversary.

But remember that cats are by nature solitary creatures. Don't expect expressions of gratitude or constant displays of affection. Just respect her, and she will be faithful to you.

Yours,

S.

I imagine Simon: her age or older, thin, his back a little bowed, walking with a cane. He's quietly elegant, his manners effortless. He subscribes to *The New York Times, The Post and Courier,* and when there was an afternoon paper he read that, too. There's a stack of books on his bedside table: some poetry, some history, a novel he's read before and wants to savor again.

Who is this man? What place did he hold in Lila Mackay's heart? Why did she include his letters in the box marked "Beatrice"? Or maybe he's dead. Yes, that would explain why she didn't include him in her list of potential caregivers.

Can't Get No Satisfaction

—◆—

He just has a couple of quick questions," says Gina when I ask her why Rick Silber has made this last-minute appointment. "before we set a wedding date."

Some clients won't go away, even after I hand them a certified copy of the divorce decree and send my usual follow-up letter. Sometimes it's not their fault—the furious ex-spouse refuses to comply with the order, has to be hauled into court to show cause why he or she shouldn't be held in contempt. But some clients have become so addicted to battle, they almost need the wounds. That kind of client will do something petty to revive the conflict, like failing to pack pajamas in the child's suitcase when the ex picks the kid up for weekend visitation, or sending the alimony check on time, but fifty dollars short.

In Rick Silber's case, there was no divorce. His wife was diagnosed with aggressive cancer midway through the litigation, and both parties signed a consent order of dismissal. Then his wife died. "It's a difficult psychological predicament," he says when he comes in. "I feel relieved not to be married to her anymore, but this . . . I can't really rejoice, and I have no right to mourn."

Please, I'm thinking, *it's late afternoon. I'm tired, and I don't want to sit around listening to you feel sorry for yourself.* This is, after all, the same man who left his wife to carry on an affair with his former graduate student, a woman almost twenty years his junior. But of course I don't say that. Instead, I muster all my empathy. "Rick, it's okay to mourn the loss of the marriage, the loss of the woman you were once happy with. Maybe you could use some therapy." He reminds me that he's been in psychoanalysis since college; that's what got him interested in psychology. "So, Gina said you had some questions?"

"You haven't congratulated me," he says.

"Gina's very happy."

"So am I, of course, but I have a few . . . some things I want to clear up before this goes any further."

"You're home free on the divorce case," I explain. "You got the certified copy of the Order of Dismissal, right?"

"Yes, but that's not it. This is a little awkward. . . . I didn't want to mention it to Gina until I'd talked to you." He fingers the spot where his goatee used to be, the goatee Gina convinced him to shave off. I see now why he wanted it: His receding chin melts into his turtleneck. "I think I need a prenup."

I'm about to launch into my speech about prenuptial agreements—what they can do, what they can't do—when I realize I have a way out. "Rick, I'm not comfortable advising you on this. I have a conflict of interest."

"But it's not like Gina's your client."

"She's my secretary, and she's my friend."

"Maybe you could just answer a few questions, and then I could draft the thing myself, save some money."

"If you want to talk about a prenup, you'll have to see another lawyer. I can give you some names."

"Jeez," he says, pouting, "I didn't realize I'd be losing my lawyer. It's not like Gina and I are fighting about anything."

"But I can't do anything that might potentially hurt her," I say.

"She's big girl," he says. "I doubt if she'd have any problem with a prenup."

"You haven't discussed it with her?"

"Like I said, I wanted to talk to you first."

I scribble three names on a piece of paper. "These are all good lawyers, but if I were you I wouldn't wait too long to talk to Gina."

"But it wouldn't be fair for her to end up with any of the money I inherited, right?"

"Rick, you're not listening. I can't advise you on this."

"At least promise me you won't say anything to Gina before I—"

"I won't, because you're going to tell her very soon. I won't let her sign anything without having someone review it."

"I guess that someone would be you," he says.

"Probably not."

"Because I just want this to be simple. I'm not trying to deny her something that's rightfully hers."

"No, I'm sure you wouldn't." I say this firmly. I give him a look that says, *If you do anything to hurt Gina, I'll hire a posse of lawyers to come after you.*

"What was that all about?" asks Gina when he's gone.

"He had some questions about the Order of Dismissal."

"He's just nervous," she says. "I keep telling him, what's to worry about? As long as we love each other, we'll be fine. What . . . you think I'm being naive, don't you?"

"I think you're in love."

"Mind if I leave now?" she asks. "It's almost five."

"Sure. I just need to make one call and then I'm done."

"He's so sweet I can hardly believe it," she says. "I know it sounds dumb, but I've never had a man give me things the way Rick does. Little presents all the time. Wait a minute, I'll show you something." When she comes back she's wearing a new suede jacket and carrying a huge red purse, the kind that shouts "Expensive!" She smiles. "I could get used to this."

Tony's still busy at the clinic. Maureen, his receptionist, insists on interrupting him despite my protests.

"It's not an emergency," I explain.

"But he said if you call, he wants to talk to you."

I hold, listening to fuzzy Muzak. When he picks up the phone he sounds tense, hurried. "What's up?"

"I just wanted to check on Beatrice."

"She's fine."

"Getting along okay with the dogs?"

"She's fine with the dogs, but I'm keeping her in the bedroom when I'm not there. She likes that big chair by the bed."

"If you were on the list, I'd let you keep her."

"What list?"

"Lila Mackay's list, remember?"

"Right."

"I know I told you I'd come back out there tonight," I say, "but I forgot about the condo Christmas party. I promised my mother I'd take her."

"Okay," he says, in a voice that doesn't sound okay.

"Maybe tomorrow night, if Shenille can stay with Mom."

"Whenever you can work me in," he says.

"Tony, I'm doing the best I can." There's a too-long silence. "You sure everything's okay?"

"I had a break-in yesterday."

"At the clinic?"

"No, the house."

"How could you have a break-in? You never lock the doors."

"Somebody left a note inside, on the kitchen counter. Wait a minute, I've got it in my pocket. . . . Here it is." He reads it to me.

What's a sensible man like you doing with a woman who won't listen to reason? Maybe you should talk some sense into your girlfriend before she does something she'll regret.

"Anything stolen?"

"That's the weird thing—nothing."

"Remember the other night, when I saw the car drive away?" Then I tell him about the note on the windshield.

"You should have said something."

"I think it's Randall Mackay. I'm surprised the dogs didn't tear him apart."

"My girls make a lot of noise, but they're all bark and no bite. This guy sounds like a lunatic. I'm going to call the sheriff."

"He's just trying to intimidate me."

"So I'm supposed to ignore somebody coming into my house?"

"The sheriff isn't going to do anything except take an incident report. Nothing's missing."

"Isn't an incident report good to have?" he asks. "In case something else—"

"You can call, but it's probably a waste of time. If it's Randall, he's just trying to get to me through you. It's a mind game."

"I don't like this kind of mind game. And what if he's *really* after you. I mean, what if he—"

"I think he's just trying to intimidate me into settling."

"Maybe he's after the cat. I could bring her here to the clinic during the day, but she won't be very happy in the back there with a bunch of other animals."

"If he wanted to hurt the cat, he's already had his chance. That's why I think he's just trying to intimidate me. . . . Best thing to do is lock the doors, leave the TV on when you're at work, the porch light on, a couple of lights inside. And maybe you could borrow an extra car? It would be good if you could leave one outside, so it looks like somebody's home. . . . Okay, I've got to get home, but I'll try to make it out there tomorrow night."

"Whenever you can work me in."

"I wish you'd stop that."

"*I* wish a lot of things, but let's not get into it."

"You're being petulant, but I love you anyway."

"I'm glad you can stay so calm about all this, because it makes *me* really nervous. . . . Anyway, see you tomorrow, if you can make it," he says.

What he doesn't know is that I'm struggling not to panic, trying to tell myself that this really is a mind game and nothing more. But I haven't forgotten what my ex-husband said: *His first wife divorced him on physical cruelty. The second one disappeared.*

Mom's sitting on the sofa in the living room, her back erect, shoulders raised as if she's trying to lift her sagging bosom. The little sequined purse she holds in her lap matches the short black dress, which is several sizes too small.

"We're going to be late!" she says.

"You just hold your horses," says Delores. "That party ain't going nowhere without you."

My mother looks me over. "It's the cocktail hour, you know. If you don't want to stand out like a sore thumb, you should change into something nicer."

"She looks plenty nice," says Delores. "Just a little tired around the eyes." But I know better than to argue with my mother. I change into a black dress—nothing revealing or sparkly like Mom's—add a string of pearls, brush my hair. The woman in the mirror looks back at me, trying her best to appear upbeat, but the shadows under her eyes betray her. I find some concealer in a bag of seldom-used makeup, lean in close to the mirror, dab it on. "Maybe some mascara, too, and some blusher," I say out loud.

"Why don't you come, too?" I ask Delores when I'm ready.

"Thanks anyway," she says. "I can't compete with you ladies. Besides"—she winks—"white people's parties are boring. Nothing but a lot of standing around talking."

The minute Mom and I step into the party room, it's clear that Delores was wrong. The place is packed, the music—the Rolling Stones—vibrating the dance floor, the disco lights swirling on the ceiling. Mom shouts in my ear, "I don't think this is our kind of party." There's a big Christmas tree in the corner, its white lights flashing in time to the music.

"We'll have one drink and go," I shout back to Mom. "You sit here while I get you something."

While I stand in line at the bar I check on her a couple of times. She's put on her social smile, that lips-closed smile that means she's politely enduring a miserable situation. "Two white wines, please," I say to the bartender. Why not let Mom have a little fun?

But when I turn around with the drinks in my hands, she's gone. "I'm *so* glad to see you," says Mrs. Furley. I recognize some other faces in this crowd—we ride the elevator up and down together, wave to each other in the parking lot—but hers is the only name I can muster.

"Have you seen my mother? She was right here—" Mom's purse is on the chair.

"No," she says. "But . . . oh, there she is! Look at her. . . . My goodness, isn't she a marvelous dancer!" In the middle of the dance floor my mother is wiggling her hips, bending toward her partner—he's white-headed, about Mom's age, and he seems quite entranced with her breasts. "If I had a figure like that," says Mrs. Furley, "I'd dance, too."

All I can do is watch. I drink my glass of wine and when the music changes to a slow dance—"Moon River," he's holding her very close—I finish off the second.

"Who's that man?" I ask Mrs. Furley.

"Edward Sand, or something like that."

"Who?" I can barely hear.

"Edward Sand, or maybe it's Shand. From Columbia. Nice man. He's the one I was telling you about. His wife passed away a year ago, and he decided he needed a change. We have a lot of ex-Columbians here, you know. He bought the penthouse apartment, so he must be fairly well off. . . . Honey, you look like you need to sit down . . . you must be working too hard."

I've never seen my mother look happier. She glides in his arms, her feet remembering dance steps from long ago.

The Whole Truth

———————

Of course Natalie Carter isn't the first client who's lied to me—far from it—but the older I get, the more I resent being fooled. It's not as if I don't give all my clients fair warning. At our first conference I always repeat the advice Gordon Houck gave me when I was just starting out as a public defender. He was the most respected lawyer in Charleston, a fellow who'd earned his reputation as a tenacious trial lawyer, working his way up in the bar without benefit of family connections. By the time I met him—he was in his seventies then—he took only a few cases, the ones he found interesting or challenging, and left the ordinary work to his son and the rest of the young lawyers in his firm. But he was a font of wisdom for neophytes like me and welcomed us to his office when we were in trouble, when we found ourselves in an ethical quandary, or hopelessly confused about an evidentiary issue. He'd invite us into his library, offer a cup of coffee, tell a few jokes to settle us down, and then ask for a summary of the facts of the case.

He'd digest this information, maybe ask a few questions, then he'd reach up and pull down a volume of cases, Southeastern 2nd , turn to the exact page of the case he knew would help—he had a photographic memory. But he balanced his mastery of the law with common sense. Once I came to him, distressed that I'd planned my whole defense around a theory that depended entirely on my client's version of events. Everything the client had told me was true; it's just that he hadn't told me everything, and I'd just discovered this mid-trial.

"Next time," said Houck, "when you meet with your client the first time, before you ask him a single question, you look him in the eye and say this: *For everything you tell me, I'm your lawyer. And for everything you* don't *tell me, I'm not your lawyer.* Ask him to repeat it back to you. Ask him if he understands it."

Gordon Houck couldn't save me from losing that case, but he helped me prepare for the inevitable sentencing. He'd gone to law school with the judge. "Ignore that gruff exterior—inside he's as soft as a baby. Your client grew up in foster homes, right? So did Judge Wilcox. Not many people know that. You have to convince him that this kid deserves a chance. It's his first offense, right? He's nineteen. I think if you do this right you can get him a Youthful Offender sentence . . . probably not probation because he's going to pay a price for going to trial . . . but you never know, you might hit Bill on a good day. Whatever happens, you get up, dust yourself off, get back in the saddle again. Believe me, I've landed on my ass plenty of times. Got plenty of bruises to show for it. You got to remember you're a lawyer—and a good one, from what I hear—but you're not a miracle worker."

Now, as I sit in my office with Natalie Carter, I try to remember that. "We have a problem," I begin. "Why don't you tell me again about your relationship with Derwood's law partner."

She shrugs, brushes a stray hair away from her forehead. "I've already told you about that."

"But you didn't tell me the whole story."

"Ken and I had a little fling, when I was still doing secretarial work for Derwood. Is he still making a big deal about that? We lived together for fifteen years afterward."

"Derwood has a letter from Ken, one of those AA confessionals—you know, where they apologize to all the people they've hurt. Ken says he's slept with you recently. Is that true?"

She bites her lower lip. "He promised me he wouldn't say anything."

"Apparently he had a change of heart."

"If Derwood can screw around with his court reporter, why can't I have some fun myself?"

"You can, but you won't get any alimony."

"It's not fair."

"No, it isn't, but it's the law in South Carolina. So, I want you to tell me again about your relationship with Ken."

"Derwood intimidated you, didn't he?"

"He caught me off guard, because you didn't tell me the whole story."

"It was just once, a couple of months ago. I swear, I think Derwood put him up to it." She starts to cry. "I guess I'll lose everything now."

"Not everything. You'll still have your share of the marital property."

"So, you won't give up on me?"

"Of course not. But from now on you have to tell me the truth. Remember what I told you when we met the first time? *For everything you tell me, I'm your lawyer. And for everything you* don't *tell me . . . .*"

I return some phone calls, put some finishing touches on a trial brief, and squeeze in a quick lunch at the coffee shop next door before my next appointment: Tina White, the mother who failed to show up in court for the DSS hearing. She looks even worse than she did the first time we met, so thin her bones seem to shine through her skin, her eyes dull with fatigue.

"Since they took my baby, I can't sleep. Can't eat neither."

"Have you eaten anything today?"

"No, ma'am. I got a ride here with a friend, had to leave early." The town where she lives, McClellanville, is at the northernmost reach of the county. "I been sittin' in the park over there across the street, till it was time to see you."

"I have some breakfast bars, some apple juice."

"That would be okay, I guess."

I can't save her from her sad life, but I can feed her. I can give her fifty dollars so she can take the bus into Charleston for her parenting class, her appointment with the pediatrician, her weekly visitation with the baby. And when we're finished I can accept her hug, hold her for a minute while she sobs, pat her on the back and say, "You'll get him back, Tina," though I'm not at all sure about that.

By the time I turn off the paved highway onto the dirt road to Tony's house, it's dark. I haven't told him for sure that I'm coming—I want to surprise him—but as a rabbit darts in front of the car and I brake too hard, it occurs to me that if I veered off this road into the marsh no one would miss me until morning. I turn on the radio, not paying attention to the news, just taking comfort in the voices. *Okay, okay,* I say to myself. *You're almost there.*

When I pull in front of the house there's an unfamiliar car beside his truck. The door's unlocked, no lights on in the living room or kitchen. "Tony?" The dogs bound toward me, barking : Susie and Sheba's contrapuntal duet, Carmen's nose-in-the air accompaniment.

"Hush, girls. It's just me. Where's Tony?" I flick on the hall light. "Tony?" There's a sound: a slow wheeze, a *thwack*. The door to the back porch.

"Shit!" he says as we collide in the darkness.

"Where did you come from?"

"I could ask the same thing," he says.

"I told you I'd try to get here."

"I just assumed you wouldn't make it," he says.

"What were you doing outside?"

"I thought I heard something."

"So you go walking around in the dark?"

"I have a flashlight." He turns it on. "See?"

"Whose car is that?"

"Belongs to my old girlfriend."

"So I guess you're busy."

He laughs. "You think there's another woman here? Sit," he says, pointing to the table. "You eaten yet?"

I shake my head. "I'm not hungry."

"I have some leftover eggplant parmesan—don't worry, I didn't make it."

"Where's the cat?"

"On the chair in the bedroom. Seems to be her favorite spot."

"So, who's the old girlfriend?"

"Oh, come on."

"I didn't realize you had any ex-girlfriends around here."

"So I guess *you're* the only one who's allowed to have a past love life?" He's turns his back to me, opens the refrigerator. "I can make a salad, too. . . ."

"I told you, I'm not hungry."

Before I can say no, he's poured two glasses of wine, set a plate of cheese and crackers in front of me. "Sit!" he says.

"What?"

"I was talking to the dogs."

The crackers are stale, the cheese rubbery, but I'm hungrier than I thought. "Who is she?"

"You're really determined to make a big deal about this, aren't you?"

"*You're* really determined not to answer my question."

"Jesus, would you give it a rest?" He gets up without touching his wine, heads toward the bedroom, the retrievers following. I finish my flip through the magazine on the table, *Veterinary Practice Today*. The beagle rests her chin on my knees.

By the time I get back to the bedroom he's asleep, a book across his chest, the cat with her back against him, paws in the air. Her eyes open for an instant, then close, as if to signal my insignificance. I turn off the bedside light, undress in the dark, slide in beside them. Beatrice turns away. "I'm sorry," I whisper, but I can't tell if he's heard me.

My sleep is deep but troubled. There's the old, bad dream: me as a child of five or six, at the beach with my parents on one of our rare family vacations. A huge wave catches me off guard, smacks the back of my head and drags me under, spinning me until I can't tell up from down. Just when I think I'll surely drown I'm thrown onto the sand. I'm grateful to be alive, but fearful ever after of that vast and unpredictable force.

In the middle of the night I wake to the sound of water running, wonder where I am, remember. He's in the bathroom. When he comes back to the bed he doesn't reach for me; from the sound of his breath—a long letting go, more than a sigh—I know he's turned away.

"You okay?" I ask.

"I didn't mean to wake you."

"You didn't. I'm sorry about last night."

"I guess jealousy is better than indifference."

"I was just surprised, that's all. You never told me about any ex-girlfriends."

"She was my high school girlfriend, a year behind me. We broke up my first semester at Clemson. She's married, three kids. Lives a mile down the highway. One of her boys was my son's best friend. When she brought her dog in this morning, she asked if she could leave the car in my parking lot for a few days—it's a Christmas present for the oldest kid; she wants it to be a surprise. So I said she could keep it over here. You told me to keep a car parked out front, remember?"

"Oh."

"So that's it. No drama." He sits up, against the headboard. "I can't go back to sleep."

I touch his hand. "I overreacted. I had a bad day."

"That's the problem," he says. "Does it ever occur to you that *I* might have a bad day?" I've never heard his voice like this. "For example, last night. I was going to tell you, but you didn't seem interested in anything but your own stuff."

"Tell me what?"

"My son called. He said he didn't want to come for Christmas."

"It happens in a lot of my custody cases, especially with teenagers. In my experience, the best way to handle it—

"I'm not asking for legal advice."

We're quiet for a minute. "I know it's hard."

"You have no idea how hard. For Jake, mostly."

"But it's awful for you, too."

"I gave in."

"So he's not coming?"

"He was supposed to come for two weeks, but he said he wanted to hang out with his friends in California. I said fine, I'll come out there."

"Is it because of me?"

"He doesn't know about you yet," he says.

"Maybe that's better."

"But I was going to tell him before he got here."

"Maybe you shouldn't say anything for a while. Until we're sure."

"What does *that* mean?"

"I'm trying to be honest."

"Okay, let's forget it for now," he says. "I'll be gone for a week, give us both a breather." He slides down next to me. There's something desperate, this time, about our lovemaking, as if we're both trying too hard. When we're finished he holds me until we fall back to sleep, until the sun creeps through the blinds.

"You're just like her," he says, pointing to the cat, who's sitting on the chair next to the bed, observing us.

"How so?"

"You're more content on your own. It's not that you don't enjoy affection, you just don't need so much of it."

"And you?"

"I'm more like a dog. I'll always be bounding up to you with my tongue hanging out," he says. "Hopelessly needy."

"Speaking of cats and dogs, who's going to take care of them . . . while you're in California?"

"My receptionist—Maureen—will come over, let them out a couple of times a day, feed them. She'll look after Beatrice, too, if you're okay with that."

"When are you leaving?"

"Friday morning."

"I'm flying to New York Thursday, to interview Mrs. Mackay's nephew, so I can't take Beatrice now, but I'll be back Friday night. Tell Maureen I'll pick Beatrice up then."

"She'll be fine here if you want to leave her," he says.

"I just don't feel right about it, if you're away."

"I thought you said you were worried about Delores."

"Delores won't be working over the weekend. I can take care of her myself. And once I've talked to the nephew, I'm pretty much finished with my investigation, so I can make a decision about Beatrice."

"I'm going to miss her. Like I said, she reminds me of you."

"Just make sure you lock the house."

"The key's hanging on a nail behind the bush to the left of the front door—remind me to show you before you leave." He kisses me. "Time for this vet to get to work, I guess."

I keep him in bed long enough to tell him about my mother and Ed Shand and their improbable reunion. "Wow," he says. "That's quite a story."

"But she doesn't know what she's doing. And that poor old guy has no idea what he's getting himself into."

"And I guess we're so much wiser?"

Maybe He's the One

"I didn't hear you come in," I say to Gina. She's in the combination bathroom/storeroom, looking for something in the cabinet where we keep our recently closed files. "You okay?"

"I ran into some traffic on the crosstown, and Rutledge was flooded."

"Yeah, it's pretty bad out there."

"I wish you wouldn't mess with this file cabinet," she says, still rifling through the drawer. "Everything's out of order."

"I try not to bother you if I can get something myself."

"But if you don't put them back the way they . . . it just makes more work for me."

"Which file are you looking for? I have a few on my desk."

"Okay, I'll try back there." She slams the drawer closed, turns around and almost knocks the coffee cup out of my hand. "Shit, would you watch what you're doing?" she says. And then, just before I'm about to give her the response she deserves, she's crying, her head collapsing on my shoulder, and I'm hugging her, patting her back. "I'm sorry. . . . I don't know what I . . ." she manages between the sobs.

"It'll be okay," I say, without knowing what "it" is. I lead her back to my office, settle her on the sofa, hand her the box of Kleenex.

"Thanks," she says, dabbing at her eyes. Her face amid the ruin of her mascara would be comical if it weren't so pathetic. "I guess he's right—I'm not acting like an adult."

"What are you talking about?"

"Rick. He says he doesn't know if I'm ready for an adult relationship."

"I'd say that's the pot calling the kettle . . ." I pause. "You want some coffee or something?"

"I'll be all right. It was a bad night." The phone's ringing, and after a few rings I hear Gina's sunny voice on the answering machine: *Our office hours are nine to five, and we close between one and two. Your call is important to us, so please leave a message and we'll get back to you as soon as possible.* "He's meeting with Larry Mantel this morning, about a prenup," she says.

I do my best to act surprised. "That's what's got you so upset?"

"It's not the prenup, exactly," she says, wiping a black rivulet of mascara off her cheek. "It's what he said about . . . I'm probably making a big deal out of nothing."

"Tell me what he said."

"He was explaining why he wants a prenup, and it all sounded reasonable, until he got to the part about women. He said his experience with women has taught him . . . Let me get this right. . . . His experience with women is that he needs to protect himself."

"That sounds like Rick."

"So I was trying to be understanding, not to overreact, and I asked him to be more specific," Gina says. "And then he launches into this, this *rant*, about his mother and his sister, his first girlfriend, a string of other girlfriends who 'betrayed' him—that was his word, 'betrayed.' And then he got around to his wife. I said something like, well, your wife probably felt pretty betrayed, too, when you left her for that other woman."

"Good point," I say.

"Which made him furious. He doesn't yell, but his face got really red and he just said in this kind of too-calm but really mean voice, 'That just goes to show you don't understand me at all.'"

"I think you understand him more than he wants to admit," I say.

"He can be really nice, and so generous, but I don't know . . . it's like he's always holding back something. . . . It's hard to explain."

"I think you should trust your instincts."

"I tried to tell him I would never betray him, but the more we talked the more I had the feeling, no matter how hard I try, I'll end up disappointing him." She's crying again, fingering the diamond on her finger. "We were talking about adopting a kid and everything."

"Really? His daughter's in her twenties."

"Yeah, I know we're too old, but I've always wanted another one, now that Carrie's all grown up." The phone's ringing again. "Anyway, sorry I was such a bitch this morning."

"I'm here if you want to talk some more."

"By the way, it was his file I was looking for, but I don't need it after all," she says. "You want another cup of coffee?"

"No, thanks. Is everything set up for New York?"

"Good to go. I'll print out your boarding pass. You're scheduled to meet with Dr. Freeman at ten on Friday morning, his apartment."

"I thought he was a poet."

"He was a professor, too, before he retired. So I guess that's why he calls himself 'Doctor.' By the way, I booked you in a really nice hotel," Gina says. "I figured Mrs. Mackay wouldn't mind some of her money going to put you up in style. If she can give a cat a whole plantation and a bundle of money, she can at least put you up in a nice hotel, don't you think? And it's practically right next door to Dr. Freeman's apartment building. Speaking of the cat, how's she doing?"

"She's at Tony's house. The dogs don't seem to bother her. But I'm going to pick her up when I get back from New York. Some weird things have happened. . . ." I tell her about the note on my windshield, and the one on Tony's kitchen counter. "I think it's Randall."

"God. No wonder you look kind of frazzled. I guess you called the sheriff."

"Tony's going to call. But nobody's hurt, nothing's stolen, and the cat's fine, so what are they going to do?"

"It was a burglary, right?"

"Probably not, because there's no evidence that whoever went in had the intent to commit a crime inside."

"Then trespassing, at least."

"Yes, but the sheriff won't take that too seriously."

"You want me to keep the cat while you're in New York?"

"I thought you said you couldn't have animals in your building."

"I'm not supposed to, but I could probably get away with it, for one night, anyway."

"I'd rather not move Beatrice around any more than necessary," I say. "Tony's receptionist is going to be going over there a couple of times a day to check on things. If it was Randall, and he wanted to harm Beatrice, he'd have done that already, don't you think?"

"But haven't you always said it's irrational to predict the behavior of irrational people?"

Ellen's daughter Mandy seems older than her eighteen years. She's tall, almost six feet, and she carries herself with a self-assurance that's unusual for someone her age as she strides down the hallway to my office, blond hair swinging. If she's gained weight from the pregnancy, it doesn't show. She declines my offer of something to drink and doesn't even want to sit down. "I don't want to waste your time," she says, her aquamarine eyes unwavering. "I know you're just doing this for my mother."

"I was there when you were born, Mandy. I feel like we're family."

"I appreciate that," she says, "but—"

"I drove your mother to the hospital that night. Your dad was out of town."

"And you've been a good friend to Mom," she says, still standing with her feet planted wide apart, as if she won't be moved. "But this doesn't have anything to do with you and Mom."

I take a chance: "Your mom would be appalled at how rude you're being. Sit down, would you?"

And she does, though with another exaggerated sigh and then a little smile that says, *Okay, I'll humor you, but don't take too long.* "I just want to make it clear that I've made up my mind," she says.

"Tell me what your plans are, then."

"I don't have it all totally figured out yet, but I just know I can handle it," she says. There's a tremor in her voice, barely audible, which she tries to cover up by talking fast.

"I notice you're not saying 'we.' What about the boy . . . what's his name?"

"Peter. He's eighteen, so he's not a *boy*. I can do this without him."

"I don't think it's so easy to raise a child alone."

She doesn't have to say what she's thinking, because I see it in her glare: *What the hell do you know about raising a child?* "Of course it won't be easy—I'm not stupid. Listen, I know you're just trying to—"

"I'm not trying to do anything except make sure you've

considered all the options, before you make a decision that will affect the rest of your life."

"I'm not getting rid of it, if that's what you're suggesting." Again those steady eyes, so full of determination, so much like her mother's.

"I'm not suggesting anything, just—"

"And I'm not giving it up for adoption, bringing a baby into the world and then *abandoning* it."

"That's a pretty strong word, don't you think?"

"But that's what it is. Walking away, avoiding your responsibilities. I'm not that kind of person."

"Of course you aren't." She's always been an A student, a star soccer player. Almost too perfect. "But maybe the most responsible thing isn't to try to take care of a baby all by yourself."

"I'm not dumb enough to get married just because I . . . I screwed up."

"Tell me about Peter."

"He's irrelevant, really, at this point."

"The father is irrelevant?"

"Well, I just mean that we're not going to be together, that's all. He'll have to help with money."

"He has money?"

"His parents do."

"But his parents aren't responsible for his child."

"I guess not, but once he's finished college, he'll be making money."

"And what about you? What about college?"

"I can take night courses at the College of Charleston when the baby's a little older," she says. "Gina was showing me the catalogue. She seems to think I can do it."

"You know Gina had a baby right after high school?"

"Yeah, she told me. She's a really cool woman, so easy to talk to."

"She's smart as hell, but somehow she hasn't managed to go back to school."

"Maybe I'm more determined than Gina."

"Nobody's more determined than Gina."

"Are you really trying to convince me to give my baby to strangers, walk away and never see her again?"

"It's a girl?"

"I don't know yet, but I hope so."

"There's such a thing as an open adoption, Mandy."

"A what?"

"The birth mother stays in contact with the child."

"I never heard of that."

"Which is my point. I understand you want to be responsible; of course you do. Just make sure you know all your options before you make a decision. Anything else would be irresponsible, don't you think?" She doesn't answer. "Okay, I want you to promise me three things before you go. One is, you'll keep up with your prenatal care. You've got an appointment with the obstetrician, right?"

"Yes."

"Second, you'll do some research on your options and prepare a summary."

"But I've already made up my mind. . . ."

"Pretend you're trying to help a friend who *hasn't* made up her mind yet."

"This sounds really dumb. But okay, I'll do it."

"And the last thing is, you'll come back in a month to talk again."

"I don't see why. . . ."

"I think you owe me one. If I hadn't gotten up in the middle of the night to drive your mother to the hospital, she'd have gone by herself, and you might have been born in the backseat of a car. So, is it a deal?"

"Okay."

"Good. I'm penciling you into my calendar right now. What day's best for you?"

I watch her as she walks back down the hall toward the elevator, hear her say, "See ya later!" to Gina in a voice that refuses to admit anything but optimism. Not everyone would hear the strain in it, but I do. I was like that once, striding out of my mother's house into the world, trying to convince myself that wits and guts could conquer anything.

I won't confront Mandy's naivete head-on, won't tell her she's a fool, that life isn't like a lump of clay you can just pound and push and manipulate into the perfect shape you want it to be. She's going to have to find that out for herself. All I can do is help her avoid a total mess, help her mend the cracks when they threaten to break her in two.

"You might want to look this over before your trip," says Gina. "It was in there—in the cat box—with the packet with the letters from that Simon guy. It's from the nephew."

The note is attached to a clipping—yellowed, folded into a small envelope—from *The New York Times Book Review*.

Dear Aunt Lila,

As you can see, my little book has attracted some notice. Your copy will arrive under separate cover. I hope you won't mind that I've stolen from your personal history with the poem "That Other Life." I've also sent a copy of the book to Simon, since "that other life" might have been his, as well. While the poem should speak for itself, I hope that you'll not take it as a reprimand but as a reminder, from someone who has made his share of mistakes, that pride and love can be quarrelsome partners. By the way, speaking of partners, you'll remember that after Jeremy died you cautioned me against self-pity and urged me to seek companionship. I'm too set in my ways, my dear Aunt, to risk another adventure in human love, but I've adopted a cat. I call her Sphinx. She's an elegant creature, a little feisty and opinionated, but she's a practical animal and she's decided she'll have to make do with this middle-aged poet.

Love always, Philip

"I googled him," Gina says. "He won a couple of awards for poetry books, but then he wrote a kids' book about a little boy whose best friend is a cat. It was a bestseller."

"So maybe he's the one," I say.

"Except that in that interview he seems like, you know, a totally New York sort of person. I can't imagine him living out on Edisto. What is it, fifty miles to the nearest bookstore?"

"There's a great little bookstore on the island. Right on the main road. And you haven't seen the house—Mrs. Mackay's—but I can imagine a poet living there. It's run-down, but it has lots of history. Even a ghost."

"I'll take your word for it."

"And anyway, she's the one who put him on the list, along with the other two. She must have thought he might be willing to move."

"She could have saved you a lot of trouble if she'd just made the choice herself," says Gina. "But at least they aren't all fighting over Beatrice," says Gina, "like the Harts fought over *him*." She points to the photo of Sherman. "And you get a free trip to New York. You could see a show, do some shopping."

"It's just overnight."

"You should have stayed through the weekend, at least, and taken the vet."

"He's going to California to see his son."

"I didn't know he had a kid," she says.

"He's thirteen."

"So it's complicated."

"Isn't it always?"

Then There's Hope

I don't need Ed Shand in my living room the night before I leave. I don't need Ed Shand in my living room *ever*. Here they are, Ed and my mother, sitting on the sofa, chatting away as if they've been together forever. He stands when I come in, extends his hand, says, "You probably don't remember me. . . ." But of course I do. I remember Ed and his wife—Roberta, wasn't it?—from Columbia. He sang in the choir. She was on the altar guild with Mom. My father couldn't stand him, probably because my mother thought he was "charming, and so accomplished." The Shands lived in a neighborhood of big houses and wide lawns only a mile away from Monroe Street, where our brick bungalow on its tiny lot looked much the same as the other bungalows that lined the street. My father hoped to cure Mom's disappointment by adding a den onto the back of the house, but the addition only made the rest of the rooms seem cramped and dark.

The Shands once invited us to a barbecue and, of course, Dad made up some excuse to avoid going, but Mom took me. As the adults sipped away on gin and tonics on the patio and the younger children shot each other with water guns, Mrs. Shand led me inside to the den, turned on the television, gave me a glass of lemonade. "Just make yourself at home," she said, which I interpreted to mean I was free to poke around in the bookcases and peruse the family photo albums, but as the party stretched into the night I wandered into the master bedroom, where I found a paperback under a stack of magazines on a bedside table: *Ten Steps to a Better Marriage*.

I sat on the king-sized bed (satiny bedspread, down pillows) to read it but by Step Four ("Never Go to Sleep Angry") I was bored, so I resumed my investigation of the premises, this time finding something infinitely more interesting in a drawer on the other side of the bed: a magazine with photos of naked men and women doing things I'd never imagined men and women could do.

What to do with this treasure? I knew my best friend Janie would kill me if I didn't show her, and maybe, I thought, her older sister could explain what was going on in the pictures. So I ripped out a few of the choicest photos, folded them several times until they fit in the pocket of my shorts, and went back to the den, where the TV was droning and my glass of lemonade had made a ring on the coffee table.

Later, when my mother insisted I "be polite to the other children," I went back outside, where the grown-ups were loudly boozy and the boys were talking about what kind of cars they would get when they were old enough to drive. I sat watching Mrs. Shand eyeing my mother as Ed told bad jokes—my mother laughing too loud, throwing her head back and showing off her thick hair and her long beautiful neck.

"I need to get home to finish my homework," I said, standing up with as much forcefulness as I could muster. I'd done my homework before we left home, and Mom knew that. She didn't argue, though. She drove home without saying anything, our silence as thick as the descending darkness. The next afternoon, as she presented me with the pictures she'd found in the pocket of my shorts in the laundry basket, she was disturbingly calm.

"Where did you get these?" she asked.

"In their bedroom."

"You shouldn't make things up."

"I swear." And so as not to waste the opportunity, I said, "Mr. Shand is disgusting. And you're disgusting, too, when you flirt with him like that."

She'd held back until then, but I'd pushed her too far, and she slapped me. I refused to cry. I wouldn't let her have the satisfaction. Now, with Ed Shand in my living room and my mother looking up at him adoringly, I'd like to slap her back.

But instead I'm shaking his hand. "Of course I remember you," I say. "Please—sit back down."

"Delores here was just telling me about your law practice," he says. "I'm not surprised that Margaret's daughter is so successful."

"It's a small practice," I say.

"She won't brag on herself," says Delores.

"I hear you have a specialty in dogs and cats," he says, smiling. He resumes his place on the sofa, his leg touching my mother's.

"One dog and one cat, so far," I say. "Would you excuse us for a moment? I need to talk to Delores."

Back in my bedroom, I close the door. "How long has he been here?"

"Just a little while. He's a nice man."

"I don't trust him."

"You think that old man can still do anything? No way," she says. "About all he can do is think about it."

"He could hurt her feelings."

"All they been doing is talking about the old days."

"Don't you think it's a little strange that he just happens to move into this building . . . all the way from Columbia?"

"He didn't even know Miz Margaret lived here. That's what he says, and he seems like a gentleman."

"I want you to promise me that you won't *ever* leave them alone together," I say. "I'll be out of town tomorrow and Friday, remember, and if anything should happen—"

"You got lots more things to worry about than your mama and that skinny old man," Delores says.

"He can't possibly think there's any future in it."

"Maybe he's got enough sense to just enjoy himself right now, not to worry himself about the future."

"But not at her expense."

"You see her in there? Happy as a lark."

"Tomorrow she might not remember his name."

"Don't take this wrong," Delores says, "but maybe you should worry about your own man problems." Before I can respond she puts her hand on my shoulder. "And don't you worry, I'll make sure he behaves himself."

It's past ten, and Tony's voice through the telephone has that gravelly, asleep-already sound.

"I woke you. I'm sorry."

"No . . . you didn't. I was just drifting off. Talk to me."

"I think Mom's lonely."

"I doubt it," he says. "She's got Delores and . . . what's her name . . . the other lady?"

"Shenille."

"And you, of course."

I can see him stretched out on the bed in his undershorts and a

T-shirt, a paperback splayed open beside him, the dogs on the floor around the bed.

"How's Beatrice?"

"She's right here next to me. The dogs are a little jealous. Susie and Sheba used to sleep with me when they were puppies, but when Carmen came I had to banish them—this isn't a three-dog bed. Now they don't understand why this other creature gets to sleep with me."

"I wonder if they feel the same way about me."

"I don't think so," he says, laughing. "They understand you're one of my species. But this cat—that's another matter."

"I hope she'll be okay until I can pick her up."

"She'll be fine. Maureen will come in the morning to let the dogs out, and then again at the end of the day."

"That's a lot of trouble."

"She doesn't mind. I return the favor with her dogs when she's out of town."

"Did you tell her about the problem?"

"I gave her a heads-up."

"Don't forget to tell her I'm hoping to get out there Friday night."

"Why not just wait until Saturday morning?"

"It's easier for me to drive out there straight from the airport. Shenille will stay with Mom until I get home."

"Whatever suits you," he says. "By the way, the gate will be locked. You have the combination, right? Bring a flashlight."

"That's a good idea—the gate, I mean."

"Remember the cat's welcome to stay here indefinitely."

"Mom will like having the cat around. It's Delores who'll be unhappy."

"Beatrice is no trouble."

"I know, but after that whole thing with Sherman, Delores has an attitude about me bringing animals home. I think she liked Sherman, but she'd never admit it."

"If she keeps working for you, she'll have to get used to the whole menagerie."

"What?"

"You, me, your mother, Delores, and Shenille. The dogs. And my son, if he'll ever come." He waits for me to say something. I can hear the cat's loud purring. "Okay, I'm sorry. I shouldn't push you. . . . So, what's this about your mother being lonely?"

"She seems like a different person with Ed Shand around—more like her old self."

"Maybe he reminds her of the essentials."

"What?"

"She might be almost eighty, but she's still a woman."

"I don't trust him."

"What's he going to do, run off with her?

"She's so vulnerable."

"You know what I think?" he says. "I think we're talking about you, not your mother."

"Don't psychoanalyze me, okay? . . . So, are you nervous, about Jake?"

"You're changing the subject. But, yes, I am."

"He's got to appreciate that you're being so flexible, changing your schedule to fly out there at the last minute."

"I don't think he sees it that way. As far as he's concerned, his parents should have been able to work things out, stay together, so that he didn't have to go back and forth."

"But you're doing your best."

"I am, but even at my best I'm still a pain in the ass."

"I disagree."

"Then there's hope," he says.

"Will you call me, let me know how it's going?"

"Text me when you're back from New York," he says, "and don't fall for the poet."

"Don't be ridiculous." Of course I won't fall for the poet. But I know what he's really worried about, and there's nothing I can say—at least nothing honest—to reassure him about that.

What Were You Thinking?

———◆———

From the air, before the plane banks and turns, I can see my condo building, the Cooper River, the bridge like some mythical creature with its gleaming white skeleton, and as we ascend, the harbor and the shimmering Atlantic, the network of creeks and rivers on the west side of town, where Tony is pouring his first cup of coffee in the little house, the dogs circling the kitchen, waiting to be let out. Beatrice doesn't like the dogs' commotion—all that juvenile eagerness—so she'll remain in his bedroom, on the unmade bed or the chair, until the kitchen is quiet again. Then she'll pad out, rub her back against his calves while he fixes her breakfast, talks to her.

He talks to the dogs, too, but with them he's relaxed, his monologue a gentle, easy patter, or, if they're being stubborn or loud, a mild half-joking reproach. With Beatrice he's more reserved. "We're just getting to know each other," he said when I pointed that out. "I don't like to be presumptuous."

"But you call her 'honey,'" I said.

"She doesn't mind a little affection," he explained, "as long as it's respectful."

I miss him already, miss the menagerie, the sweet chaos of his cottage, but could I live with him there—or anywhere? It isn't just the logistical challenge, the merging of two people with busy careers. There's also my mother, and the teenager I haven't even met. The thought of all of us together, even for a weekend, unnerves me. *We'll work it all out,* Tony says. Maybe he's right, but that's almost exactly what Joe Baynard said before our wedding, when I panicked that his family wouldn't like me. I realize now what I didn't understand then: What I really feared was that I couldn't be the wife Joe needed, and that we were both fooling ourselves to think I could be.

The man next to me—young, smelling like last night's whiskey—has fallen asleep, his mouth open. When his head flops onto my shoulder, I shift assertively in my seat, and he wakes up. "Oh, sorry," he says groggily. And then, "You from Charleston?" I nod. "Going to the big city for some fun?"

"Business," I say, reaching for my briefcase.

Gina has made a copy of what she calls "the cat diary" so that I can finish reading it. I'm accustomed to reviewing documents, scanning them for relevant information, making notes for later reference. But this is so unlike anything I usually come across in my files, these observations of a woman in the guise of her beloved pet, a woman who seems to inhabit the soul of her cat:

> *My favorite view is from the east window of the parlor. Up here, I can see the brick path down to the river, the two big oaks on either side, the moss hanging from their limbs, the lawn and the water beyond. The windowsill's just wide enough for me (yes, I've put on a little weight) to lie comfortably, and on a sunny day this spot is so warm it puts me to sleep. But the best time for spotting birds is at dusk, when my vision is*

keenest. Ah, this is heaven! She'll call me soon, coax me down to the
basement apartment, where I'll sit in her lap while she reads me a
story.

And this cat's a student of history:

Sometimes I can smell the sweat of the ones who toiled here, the human
beings who lived in the one-room cabins (long gone) behind the "big
house," who bent over the rows of cotton from dawn to dusk; the women
who cooked in the old kitchen—some drunk Yankee burned it down
during the war, but you can see the remains of its foundation in the side
yard—and hauled the food up to the dining room; the girl who made
the beds and swept the floors and once got a whipping for sampling the
French perfume on her lady's dressing table.
  Such elegance. And such untold suffering, to maintain it.

And the cat observes her owner with cold objectivity:

Hard to imagine she was once a beauty, this bony old woman with the
whispy white hair she doesn't bother to cut, bundled in a sort of bird's
nest with bobby pins.

But in the last few entries of the diary, Lila Mackay abandons the
voice of the cat. The notes are disjointed, the words spilling down
the pages as if the author's falling, the ink smeared:

Make peace with myself. Mistakes. Worse than. Done is done.
  Useless, looking back. But the ghost? Lila, he says. Lila. Abandoned
trust.
  In the end, what's left of love? Beatrice. Warm weight in my lap.

Before I close my eyes the plane soars into the clouds, an infinite blankness. Down there, I know, Delores reminds my mother to use her napkin, coaxes her to eat another bite of scrambled eggs. Gina sweats on the treadmill, running with all her might, imagining herself with thinner thighs, a tighter butt. My friend Ellen dresses for a day in court—dons a new suit, adds a scarf. Looks in the mirror expecting to see a prosecutor and sees, instead, a grandmother.

And there's Beatrice. *What's left of love.*

Those yellow eyes, so steady. Are they accusing me?

Abandoned trust.

The lobby of the hotel is white marble and mirrors, minimalist. A couple of chairs on one side, more like sculptures than furniture—nothing you would want to sit in—and the reception desk along the opposite wall, an expanse of gleaming marble. *Too clean,* I think, *for commerce.* A young woman stands behind it. She's as exquisite as the white orchid in the vases behind her. I give her my credit card. She smiles a marble kind of smile. "Your room overlooks the park," she says.

I can hear Gina: *It's just for one night, so you might as well live it up. And there's great shopping right next door.* I unpack, hang my things in the closet. I've brought too much, and in the elegant simplicity of this room all my clothes seem dowdy. Maybe I *should* go shopping. Gina again: *Why don't you treat yourself, just this once?*

I set out with good intentions, but once inside the Time Warner Center I panic, rush past the ground-floor shops—Hugo Boss, Cole Haan; not in my league—and take the escalator to the second floor, where the offerings are less expensive but the stores more crowded. I try on a few things, reject all but one, buy it—more because I don't want to admit defeat than because I like it. On the way back down, my new dress practically screams from the bag: *What were you thinking?* It's cherry red, a slinky knit, too short for court, too loud for an interview with a poet.

Across the street, the park's a refuge. It's cold, but the sun has snapped the day alive with runners, babies in strollers, people walking their dogs, all the adults zipped up in practical black and gray, the babies and the fancy little dogs in fashionable outfits.

"Some people have too much money for their own good," grumbles the old man at the other end of the bench.

I smile a noncommittal *I don't really feel like talking* smile, but he's determined: "There are children in this city who don't have enough to eat, and look at that!" He points to a fluffy little dog sporting a plaid vest, prancing ahead of its owner. "What a country!" He takes equal offense at the cell phone ringing in my purse. "And *those* things! It's an insult to the peace-loving populace!"

I get up, walk away, fish for the phone. "Gina?"

"What's that noise?" she asks.

"I'm in Central Park."

"I hate to bother you, but they want to do an interview."

"Who wants to do an interview?"

"You remember that reporter from the *Post and Courier* who did the story about pet custody cases? She wrote a follow-up—about the cat case—in this morning's paper. I guess you didn't see it."

"How does she know about the cat case?"

"They're doing a profile of Judge Clarkson, I guess because he's retiring, and he was talking about the unusual cases that come through the Probate Court, and he mentioned the cat case. So the reporter called here, and you were busy with a client, so I gave her a little background. She left a message for you, but I forgot to give it to you before you left and—"

"Slow down."

"And now there's this guy calling from CNN."

"I'm not getting this.

"She—the reporter from the paper here—asked me if you were developing a specialty in animal law. And I must have said yes."

This stops me in my tracks. "Oh, sorry, miss," says the woman who runs into me with a stroller.

"I knew you'd be mad," says Gina, "but I don't see how this could hurt anything."

"Send me the article. And what were you saying about CNN?"

"The guy who called is in Atlanta, but when I told him you were in New York, he said, great, he'd arrange the interview—"

"Absolutely not."

"I gave him your number."

"We're going to have a talk about this when I get back."

"What are you doing in the park, anyway? Dr. Freeman's expecting you at five. Who goes to the Big Apple and hangs out in a park?"

"It's nice here. Lots of trees."

"You like the hotel?"

"It's fine."

"Pretty cool to have a TV in the bathroom, huh? You can take a bath and watch a movie."

"I don't take baths."

But when I get back to the hotel that's exactly what I do. On the bathroom counter there's a collection of fancy soap, shampoo, and lotion. Lavender body wash, bath oil in little lavender-colored pods, a loofah, a miniature pumice stone. A coupon for 15 percent off on a $300 full-body massage.

I sink into the water, close my eyes, breathe the steam. The warmth takes me back to the apartment with Joe, such a long time ago, the second-floor apartment in the old house on Rutledge Avenue, the claw-footed tub in the dingy bathroom. We both preferred showers, but there was only a handheld sprayer, and the shower curtain wouldn't close all the way, so we took turns sitting in the tub, one of us bathing while the other aimed the spray. And when I'd had an especially stressful day in court he'd run a hot bath with bubbles, settle me in it, bring me a glass of wine. That bathroom was so small the toilet was practically under the sink, but he made it seem like a palace.

Once, just before our divorce, when we were arguing all the time, he said, "Maybe you should take a hot bath."

"If you could go back, do it over, would you?" Ellen asked me once a couple of months ago.

"I'd still be me, and he'd still be Joe."

"Which wasn't so terrible, was it?"

"Things would have gotten a lot worse if we'd stayed together," I said.

"Maybe you'd have matured. You're both decent people with lots of love to give."

"He still wants what he always wanted. The house on Meeting Street, the Yacht Club, etc. I would have made him miserable."

"And Susan makes him happy?" Ellen said.

"That has nothing to do with it."

"I'm just saying—"

"What *are* you saying?"

"Just that, you know, relationships evolve," she said. "And you know what I think? I think all your nonsense about not making him happy is . . . well, it's just not *honest*. It's a cop-out. What you really mean is, he wouldn't have made *you* happy. You married him, and then you changed your mind. . . . Am I onto something?"

"Let's drop it, okay?"

The hot bath has made me pleasantly woozy, so I stretch out on the bed, close my eyes. But the noise of the city won't let me rest, the sirens, the horns, all of them setting off my mental alarm: *Is Beatrice okay? And what about Mom?* When my cell phone rings, the familiar sound is a relief.

It's CNN, someone named Jillian who sounds very young, very nervous. It's such a lucky coincidence, she says, that I happen to be in the city at the same time she's working on "this in-depth, really fascinating piece about lawyers who advocate for animals," and when I stop her, explain that my experience in this area is really quite limited, she doesn't seem at all disappointed, she prattles on and on— "We just want a human face behind the story"—until before I know it I've agreed to "a very quick video session that won't take more than ten minutes," tomorrow morning. Do I mind coming to the studio? It's not far from the hotel. I want to say, *No, I'm sorry, I don't have time,* but her voice is so plaintive—she wants this so much, she needs it, this young woman at the beginning of her career—that I agree.

Just before I hang up she says, "Oh, and when you come to the reception desk, ask for Brian Hancock. He'll be doing the interview. I'm just an intern."

The Human Parade

The doorman nods. "Fifth floor, then it's down the hall on your left, last apartment on that end. If he's listening to his music he won't hear the doorbell. Just keep ringing. He's there." And indeed, as I stand outside Apt 5L, I can hear a *Brandenburg Concerto*. I press the button, press it again.

"Coming! Coming!" Dr. Freeman yells, flinging the door open. He's in his bathrobe, his long gray hair matted on one side, standing out like a fan on the other. "I was just . . . Won't be a minute. Don't try to make friends with the Sphinx," he points to the gray cat on the sofa. "He doesn't tolerate intrusions."

I'm glad to have this time to look around. The furniture's drab, stuff that might have been fashionable in the fifties but now looks bleak and worn. There's a half-dead ficus in one corner. The kitchen's tiny, dingy but uncluttered: not much cooking goes on there. Except for an old upright piano—the bench piled high with what must be several months' worth of *The New York Times*—all the available wall space is taken up with bookshelves. This is his obsession: poetry, hundreds of volumes in alphabetical order. When I reach up for one of the books, the cat lets out an unfriendly "Yee-ow," as if to say *Keep your hands to yourself!*

"You're welcome to borrow that if you like," Dr. Freeman says behind me. "But please sign for it and return it." He points to a notebook at one end of the dining room table. He's dressed now, in corduroy slacks and a tweed jacket, his hair combed back away from his face but still unruly, like smoke after an explosion.

"No, thank you, I won't have time to do any reading while I'm here."

"Oh, my dear," he says, "one should always take time for poetry. Would you like something to drink? I'm afraid my offerings are rather limited: tea or scotch. Or water, if you'd prefer." I opt for water. He pours himself a generous dose of single malt. "But you've come on a mission, so let's get our business done and then we'll go across the street for some nice Italian. She would like that."

"Excuse me?"

"My aunt, the one who brings us together! Lila was always worried I might turn into a hermit. I had to remind her that being alone is different from being lonely. Who could be lonely, with all these friends?" He gestures toward the books. "Sure you wouldn't like some scotch? Our reservation isn't until six."

I take the scotch, and though Dr. Freeman insists that I should interrupt him if I have any questions, he tells me more in his rambling monologue than I would ever learn from the list of questions I've prepared. He talks and talks, refilling his glass as he goes, sometimes rising and walking around the room, glass in hand, once accidentally splashing a little toward the cat, who's lying on one end of the sofa. Now and then he laughs at his own story, throwing his head back with a high-pitched howl, and even then the cat remains unperturbed, as if he's heard this before.

"Lila was like a mother to me," he says. "My own mother—her sister—did her best to change me. She called me her 'sissy boy,' sent me to a therapist. Lila was appalled. She was quite open-minded about such matters, for her time. That's how I came to spend so much time in South Carolina, mostly in the summertime. But I didn't get along with Randall, who teased me mercilessly. . . . But I'll come back to Randall.

"Lila encouraged my writing," he continues. "Offered to pay my tuition at Columbia, but I got a scholarship. And later, after I'd gotten the job at NYU, she helped me with the down payment on this apartment. She sent me a generous check every Christmas. I had my salary, but her contributions allowed me to spend my summers traveling, writing. She was my patron, not just financially, but emotionally. So different from my parents, who wanted me to go into the law, or medicine." He fills our glasses again. "Both honorable professions, to be sure, but not what I wanted. Lila understood that. I owe her my life, really. She gave me my independence. 'Follow your heart,' she said when I told her about Jeremy. We were together for twenty years. But that is the irony, you see. The same woman who encouraged me to live my life as I pleased, this woman now wants to control me. From the grave."

"I don't understand."

He's agitated now, sweating. The cat yawns. "She knew how much I love this city. My life is here. How could she ask me to give it up? I'm retired, but—"

"Maybe she thought she'd be doing you a favor, letting you live in the house where you spent so many happy summers." Why do I feel the need to defend her, this woman I never knew? "And besides, she named two other people, so maybe she didn't want you to feel pressured."

"Indeed." He smiles. "But don't you see? It's almost like a

game. She sets up this trust, all this money and property tied up for a *cat*."

"But you like cats, obviously."

"I like cats, yes. However, should I predecease the Sphinx here, I've arranged for him to live with one of my former students. The Sphinx, as mysterious as he may seem, is a creature with simple needs. He doesn't require an apartment on West Sixtieth with a doorman. My assets will go to charity. . . . No, as I was saying, Lila is playing a game with us. With *you*."

"She didn't even know me. She left the job of choosing Beatrice's caregiver to the probate judge in Charleston, but he—"

"Yes, yes, you explained all that in your letter. But this is no accident, this conversation. If the good judge hadn't shirked his responsibility, I'd be having it with *him*. And wherever she is—granted, I'm no believer, but she's listening—Lila hears me say, 'No, I'm sorry, I won't do it.' And she knows how guilty I feel." He looks at his watch. "One more thing before we go to dinner—so that you don't agonize over your decision too much—in her later years, my aunt always felt unappreciated."

"I suppose that often happens to old people."

"No, no . . . What I mean is, she wanted what we all want, what is at the heart of all our striving, all our loving . . . perhaps all our poetry. . . . She wanted to be *understood*." He stands, takes my empty glass. "This isn't about who's best for the cat, it's about Lila. She set up this legal instrument as a game, the object of which—remember?—is to find the caregiver who can provide the same 'emotional environment'—those were her words, weren't they?—as she provided for Beatrice. So all this is really about understanding Lila. How she lived, how she loved, what mattered to her. In short, *who she was*. When you understand *her*, then you'll make the best choice."

"But her son claims she was demented."

Dr. Freeman laughs again. "Not in the slightest. She did all this on purpose. She was bound and determined that we'd pay attention to her, even in death! . . . Now, my dear, shall we dine?"

"This was Lila's favorite restaurant," he says as the maître d' leads us to a table. "She insisted on sitting near the window, where she could watch the human parade. That's what she called it, 'the human parade.' She was like a child sometimes, enormously curious. She could entertain herself just watching the passersby. . . . At the museum once—I think it was the Met; yes, we were in the American wing—she struck up a conversation with a total stranger, an art student, invited her to join us for dinner."

"The usual, Dr. Freeman?" asks the waiter. "For you and Mademoiselle?"

"If she'll trust my judgment," he says, but doesn't wait for my answer. "And a bottle of the sauvignon blanc, please."

"I'm surprised," I say. "I had the impression she was a loner."

"In her last years, yes, because she insisted on staying in that house—rather remote, don't you think? So many of her friends were too old and frail to visit. But in her younger days she was quite the hostess . . . always surrounded herself with the most interesting people. Writers and artists, as long as they weren't pretentious—she couldn't abide pretentious people—and even a lawyer or two every now and then." He smiles. "She'd say, 'I'm having one of my potluck parties. She'd invite six people, tell each to bring another guest or two and something for the table, she didn't care who or what, as long as the people were interesting and the dish was edible. But they were almost never Verner's kind of people."

"Her husband?"

"Yes. Poor Verner. She overwhelmed him. He was a genius with money—commodities, I think—but socially, and in every other respect, quite unimaginative. He spent most of his time at their house in Charleston."

"So it wasn't a happy marriage?"

"She realized early on, I think, that she could maintain the arrangement as long as they didn't spend too much time together. She had what she wanted. She had her place on Edisto and the money to keep it up. Her books and her parties. And Randall, though God knows *that* didn't turn out well."

I tell Dr. Freeman about my encounters with Randall. "He scares me."

"I haven't seen him in years. Have no desire to. He's made it very clear that he despises me. . . . But he is, like all of us, the product of his upbringing. Lila chose her life at Oak Bluff over Randall." He sips his wine. "But I don't mean to sound so harsh. A toast to her! To Lila, who brought us together!"

I lift my glass. "Why did she have to choose between the plantation and her son?"

"By about age twelve he was already getting into trouble. Petty theft, minor vandalism. Verner realized Lila couldn't manage him, put him in private school in Charleston. She would come into town on weekends, but most of the time she stayed on the island. She wouldn't consider moving back to town. Who knows, perhaps if she had . . . Randall would be different."

"You know he's threatening to set the trust aside?"

"I'm not surprised. I'm sure he's furious."

"But it would be an uphill battle," I say, "and if he loses, he forfeits his share."

"You should be very wary of Randall. You know about the incident with her bank account? . . . No, how could you—she didn't take any legal action against him. Some time ago . . . after Verner died, about fifteen years ago, I think, Randall offered to help her with her bookkeeping. It wasn't that she was incapable, just that financial matters always bored her. She should have hired someone, but she didn't want to spend the money. She was so generous toward others, but when it came to her own needs, she could be irrational. . . . In any event, Randall convinced her to add his name to her investment account, her checking account. He paid her bills. I suppose she was relieved to have someone handle things, and perhaps she was pleased that Randall was paying some attention to her, after all those years of emotional distance. But it was an extremely unwise decision. By the time she caught on, Randall had withdrawn almost a hundred thousand dollars. He had the gall to claim she'd agreed to pay him a salary!"

"How do you know she didn't?"

"Because she told me she didn't, and there was nothing wrong with her memory. Nothing at all. She should have taken him to court, but I think she was embarrassed. That was the end of their relationship."

"Who else knows about this?"

"Her stockbroker, I suppose. Perhaps that lawyer of hers, on Edisto."

"He's dead."

"Then maybe the judge."

"He hasn't mentioned it."

"As I said, she was probably embarrassed. She wouldn't have wanted a scandal. And I think she felt some guilt about Randall, about not being much of a mother to him. I hope you like the fish. Always her favorite. But my dear, you seem troubled. Perhaps I've told you more than you wanted to know."

He doesn't wait for me to answer. "When you're as old as I am," he says, "you'll understand that everyone has a secret history. The woman I knew, when I spent those summers on Edisto, was so charming, so witty, with such a wide-ranging intelligence, enormously open-minded. But in the end she was essentially alone, an unhappy old woman . . . living with her cat and her regrets."

"She had Gail, the caretaker."

"Gail can run a tractor, but she couldn't have been much of a soul mate for someone like Lila."

"She's very good with Beatrice."

"Lila read to that cat every day. I know it seems ridiculous, but I saw it myself, the last time I visited—Beatrice in her lap, purring away as Lila read to her. Theirs was a rare companionship, creatures of different species, but with similar sensitivities."

"What about Katherine Harleston? The librarian."

"I met her only once. My impression was that Lila did more for Katherine than Katherine did for Lila. A lopsided friendship."

"But Lila obviously trusted her."

"I know this will sound preposterous, but it's another example of Lila's desire to control. She never liked Katherine's husband. . . . I've forgotten his name."

"Hugh."

"Yes. Never met him, but I know that Lila advised her to leave him. Perhaps if you choose Katherine, she will."

We're silent as we finish the main course, watching the human parade: a woman in fake fur and five-inch heels lugging two huge shopping bags; a grizzled old man, barely moving, back bent, pushing a cart full of empty cans; a twentyish girl in a black T-shirt and tights, arms covered with tattoos, oblivious to the cold.

"I'm afraid I haven't helped you much," he says.

"You've been very generous with your time. By the way, she left a box full of personal things. Letters, a diary. Someone in the family should have it."

He smiles. "But we were talking about the cat—"

"I'll make sure she's safe and cared for."

"Perhaps you should take her yourself," he says.

"I can't do that."

"But didn't she leave open that possibility . . . not *you* specifically, of course, but 'any other suitable person'?"

"I have a law practice. I can't move to Edisto." The waiter removes the dinner plates, describes the desserts, but I decline. "It's so strange. I never met Lila Mackay, but . . . I have this awful feeling I'm letting her down."

"My aunt broke many hearts! Even dear Simon, who understood her better than anyone, couldn't—"

"Simon?"

"Her first love."

"That must be the one whose letters are in the box. But why would she—"

"She could be quite sentimental, my aunt, even about her failures. . . . No, of course not, this is my treat." He pays the bill, helps me with my coat. "We'll have some coffee, back at my place, and I'll tell you the story. . . . What a smashing dress! That red!"

It's only as we're stepping outside that I realize he isn't talking about some stranger in the human parade. He's talking about me.

Simon

⸺◆⸺

Dr. Freeman makes a pot of coffee, strong. I drink two cups—I shouldn't, I'll be up all night—while he talks. The Sphinx lies between us on the sofa. Every now and then Dr. Freeman reaches out to stroke his back, a gesture the cat acknowledges with a blink or a twitch. It's clear he's accustomed to long stories.

"I'll never truly understand what happened between them—Lila and Simon Witowski. I once accused Lila of anti-Semitism, which she denied, of course—you know, the old 'I have many Jewish friends' defense—but I think, to give her the benefit of the doubt, it was more a matter of class. If that's more forgivable. In any event, his father was a tailor, Polish-born, I believe. He had a shop in downtown Charleston; that's how she met him—Simon, I mean. Her father sent her to pick up some trousers he'd left to be hemmed, but she got there half an hour after the shop had closed. She saw this boy inside—a teenager, sweeping. She was determined to pick up the pants, and banged on the door. He opened up—what else could he do? She was a *force*, my aunt, not to be ignored. Of course, she struck up a conversation. They were both seniors in high school, he at the public school, she at . . . what's that girls' school? Ashley something. Yes, Ashley Hall.

"Simon had a relative here in the city, who owned a bookstore on East Eighty-third. It's long gone now, but Simon spent several summers working there. That's how he ended up at City College. And from there he got a job at a small press, also long gone, swallowed up by some conglomerate. Lila was at Vassar by then, and she would come into the city on weekends. He introduced her to his literary friends. I have a photo of them somewhere. He was tall and bony, curly black hair, always a serious expression. . . . She wasn't beautiful, but pretty enough in an unself-conscious way, and she had those spirited, dark eyes. She was intellectually . . . how shall I say it? Immensely curious about everything and everybody. And so vivacious. I'm sure Simon found her irresistible.

"As I said, I'll never know what really happened between them, whether she was just leading him on or they had a falling-out, but all of a sudden she was engaged to Verner. They married and settled in Charleston. Once—it was probably ten years ago, one of Lila's last visits here—I asked her what happened. She seemed offended, as if I'd trespassed onto her private territory, but she said Verner understood the way she felt about Edisto, the house at Oak Bluff. When she met him, her parents were planning to sell it; they didn't have the money to keep it up. He was a shrewd businessman, Verner, not a bad man, but nothing like Lila in temperament. A man of facts and figures. Very quiet, almost brooding. And Lila so lively! I suppose that's what attracted him in the beginning, but it wasn't a happy marriage. As the years went by, Lila spent more and more time at Oak Bluff.

"I was always rather mystified by her obsession with the place. So difficult to maintain, that big old house, practically impossible to keep up, even with plenty of money! As she grew older I tried to convince her to sell it, buy something more practical in Charleston. But she wouldn't hear of it. To her it was much more than just real estate. She was connected to it—to the whole island, really—in a way that was almost . . . dare I say, *spiritual*. She would talk rapturously about the ocean, the river, the creek, the tides. She was an amateur naturalist, knew the names and habits of every bird. And then there was the human history, which she knew so well. She read extensively, all the available texts, but she also collected oral histories, the stories of the old-timers—black and white. She was sentimental about the place, but realistic about its history.

"But back to Simon. His father the tailor was in bad health, closed the shop. His mother begged him to come home, so Simon left New York and opened a bookstore on King Street. It was successful for many years. . . . . What was it called? The Book Nook. Yes, that's it. You remember it?"

"Of course," I say. "It's been closed for years."

"Then you must remember *him*. . . . What energy he had, it was infectious. I first went there when I was about eight, I think. It was such a pleasure, that shop. His made his customers feel as if they were his special guests. The place was alive with his enthusiasm. He had an old sofa and a couple of easy chairs. And cats! There was always a cat, sometimes more than one. If you wanted to be left alone to browse the shelves, fine. If you wanted suggestions, he'd give them."

"And I remember his cats."

"Simon lived and breathed books. He knew a great many writers from his New York days, and he lured them to Charleston for readings. The place was packed then, all the chairs taken, standing room only!"

"I went to some of those readings, when I had time," I say.

"But he wasn't much of a businessman. Little by little the debts caught up with him and he had to close. But I'm digressing. . . .

You're interested in his relationship with Lila, of course. I can only tell you what I suspect: that they remained lovers, though she never confessed to it in so many words. I often wondered why, after Verner died, she didn't marry Simon. But by then they were in their sixties, and my aunt . . . How shall I say this? If she had a fatal flaw, it was hubris. She couldn't admit that she'd made the wrong choice. But I'm being judgmental. We may try, but do we ever truly understand the inner lives of those we love?

"No more coffee? Perhaps some cognac? What I'm trying to say—you see, I'm a poet, but as inarticulate as anyone, really, about these matters—is that to love another is the most noble of human endeavors, and the most difficult. . . . To do it well: a rare thing. It must begin with understanding, with empathy, and proceed with great patience to acceptance. A rare thing, indeed.

"I sent Simon a copy of my fourth book, because I'd borrowed from their story, his and Lila's. It was just the one poem, but I thought it only right to share it with him. He thanked me, but I felt I'd somehow offended him, appropriated his life, his emotions. We writers do that, you know, almost without thinking. Of course, he never discussed any of this with me—we were just acquaintances. Almost everything I knew about him came through Lila, or my mother. He wrote a polite, cursory note thanking me for the book. That was many years ago, and we didn't correspond afterward, or see each other again. And Lila, in those last years, never mentioned him. But how strange, now, that Simon should come alive for me again! And you.

"Here *you* are . . . yesterday only a name to me, today—shall I presume to say—a friend? Lila would like this so much, that we've become friends!"

Going to the Dogs

———◆———

He's movie-star handsome, this CNN reporter, Brian Hancock, as if he might not really be a reporter, but playing the part of one. Strong-jawed, suspiciously tan for this time of year. He looks familiar; maybe I've seen him on TV. "This shouldn't take too long. We'll get right to it," he says. The cameraman's right behind him. "I thought, since you didn't bring the cat, we'd do this in the park. We can work in some dog shots."

I hate cameras. *Some girls just aren't photogenic,* my mother used to say when I'd bring home the sample photos from school, *but you could at least try to* smile. She'd never pay for an 8-by-10, and only once or twice did she purchase the smaller ones, for my grandparents. In my elementary school yearbooks my face was entirely forgettable. In my high school senior photos—why did I have to share a page with the homecoming queen?—my hair looked flat, my eyes dull, and the smile I attempted seemed not my own, but an expression I'd borrowed from someone else. We were supposed to pose with a prop, something that would "express your personality, your interests." I chose a book. I was a reader, wasn't I? I grabbed a book off the shelf in my room. When I saw the photo in the yearbook I was horrified. I was holding *The Scarlet Letter* against my chest.

"Let's do a couple of shots with those dogs in the background," Brian Hancock says to the cameraman. The cameraman adjusts my coat collar, brushes a strand of hair away from my cheek. "And I like the briefcase, so let's make sure you get that in, okay?"

People are starting to crowd around. They're mostly quiet, respectful of this ritual, but I hear one woman say to another, "She could use a little makeup, doncha think? . . . I dunno, some kind of lawyer, I guess."

Brian Hancock's lead-in is smooth: *If you're one of this country's approximately fifty million dog owners, or if like forty-six million others you share your home with a cat, we probably don't have to convince you that animals need love and give back plenty in return. But do they need lawyers? Sarah Baynard is one of Charleston, South Carolina's premier attorneys. She's represented accused murderers and handled high-profile divorces, but now she's expanded her client list to include a schnauzer and a cat. Sarah, what drew you to this new specialty?*

I correct him, insist that I don't really specialize in animal cases, but acknowledge that I have a reputation for taking on tough cases. "I was appointed to represent the schnauzer, Sherman, because the judge felt the dog needed someone to protect his interests," I explain. "I'm pleased to say he's now back with his family and thriving, and I'm certain that once I'm finished with my investigation, Beatrice the cat will be in good hands, too." I talk a little bit about pet trusts. And yes, I say, I find the whole field of animal rights fascinating, and while I'm certainly no expert, I'm learning.

"It went okay, I guess," I tell Gina when I call her from the airport. "Anything going on?"

"Nothing urgent. Derwood Carter's requested a final hearing. Natalie's kind of upset. I guess she thought he was going to settle."

"Why don't you start working on a witness list with her. And I need you to do something else, a little detective work. You remember that bookshop on King Street, the Book Nook? The fellow who owned it, Simon Witowski, I don't know if he's still alive, but if he is, I want to find him. It's for the cat case."

"I'll work on it. I left the file for the Farrell adoption on your desk. Everything's ready to go. Ten o'clock Monday morning."

"Anything else?"

"Just some discovery requests in the Carlisle case and a whiny letter from Richard Schultz, complaining that he gave away too much, that you pressured him into the agreement."

"That's baloney. He's the one who wanted to get it over with."

"You sound tired."

"I hate airports. The line for security was horrible. . . . Would you do me a favor? My battery's low. Call Delores and remind her that I won't be home until around seven. I'm going out to Tony's to pick up Beatrice."

"He's evicting her?"

"No, but he's in California, with his son. It was kind of a last-minute thing."

"I can't wait to see it," says Gina.

"The cat?"

"No, the CNN thing."

I'm waiting at the gate in Newark, napping before my flight leaves, when I hear my own voice, and for a second or two I ignore it—I must be dreaming—but it's insistent, and when I open my eyes I see myself on the TV monitor, in Central Park with Brian Hancock. I'm surprised at how relaxed I seem, but somehow my protestations about not really having a specialty in animal cases, not being an expert—"I've only handled these two cases so far"—haven't made it into the final cut. And the interview ends with something that had caught me off guard. It was an obvious question, one I should have anticipated. I can't quite hear the words now, but I watch them scroll across the bottom of the screen.

Brian Hancock: *You have a pet of your own?*

My moment of hesitation has been edited out, so I sound happy about the answer:

Sarah Baynard*: I just adopted a dog. She's a beagle mix. Carmen. We'll have some adjusting to do, both of us, but that's what a relationship is all about, isn't it?*

The woman beside me elbows the man sitting next to her: "Ridiculous, isn't it? She must have run out of clients . . . so she goes to the dogs!" I turn my head away so she won't recognize me, pretend to be absorbed in my magazine. She goes on: "Don't you just hate them—the damn lawyers?"

I text Tony: *Hope all is going well there. On my way home. Will pick up Beatrice tonight. Miss you.*

He doesn't text back.

Where's Beatrice?

———◆———

The tide's high, the wind strong from the east, the water lapping over the marsh grass and splashing onto the dirt road in front of my Toyota. The headlights, even on high beam, hardly penetrate the fog. *Slow*, I tell myself. *Slow, and you'll be fine.*

At the edge of Tony's property the metal gate seems to appear out of nowhere and I hit the brakes, shaken. *He told you it would be locked, remember?* When I finally get the combination to work and slip the chain off the lock, the wind catches the gate, sends it swinging away from me, screeching on its hinges.

Where's the car that belongs to his ex-girlfriend? It's gone. The house is dark. I grope for the key. I can hear the dogs barking on the other side of the door. "Hey, girls, calm down. It's me." I find the light switch in the hall. The dogs take turns licking my hands, dancing around me. I almost trip over Carmen. "Okay, okay. Settle down. Where's Beatrice?" Her carrier's not in its usual spot on the counter by the telephone.

The dogs follow me back to Tony's bedroom. "Beatrice?" She's not on the bed or the easy chair. "Beatrice?" Susie and Sheba bark at the sound of her name. Carmen presses her nose against the back of my knee, whimpers. I reach around, stroke her under her chin. The dogs follow me as I check the back porch, make another round through the bedrooms, the bathroom, even open the closets, just in case. My call to Tony goes to voice mail.

I'm about to dial the sheriff when I see the note on the refrigerator door, sharing a magnet with a photo of Tony's son. *Sally—Beatrice is okay. Call me, I'll explain. Maureen.* Tony's receptionist hasn't left a number, and of course the clinic's closed. I try Tony again, leave another message.

The retrievers have settled down but Carmen's whimpering. I sit for a minute at the kitchen table, stroking her under her chin. "I can't stay, honey. Not tonight." When I try to leave she lifts her head and howls—a desperate wailing that sounds almost human—and she won't stop until I reach for her leash on the hook beside the front door. She holds her head still while I attach it to her collar, as if she knows I need all the help I can get.

The beagle and I share the elevator with a man I remember from the home owners' party. *He's too young for this place,* I had thought. Maybe he was thinking the same thing about me. I chose this place because it was quiet, blessedly devoid of college kids and their all-night parties, but the longer I live here the more it seems like a retirement home.

"I hope you found your mother!" He smiles. He's handsome, black hair graying at the temples, dark eyes, skin a deep bronze. There's a stethoscope around his neck. At the party he'd tried to start a conversation, but I was too busy looking for Mom.

"Yes. She didn't go far."

"Nice dog," he says, nodding at Carmen. When the doors open

he turns, doesn't notice when the stethoscope falls to the floor. I call after him, "Wait, you dropped—"

"Thanks . . . Long day." Then his eyes snap to attention. " Aren't you . . . You're the lawyer for the cat, right? I saw you on CNN."

The doors close before I have a chance to answer.

What I need tonight is what I never have anymore—the apartment to myself. Even in those first few months after the divorce, when it felt strange not to see Joe's face across the dinner table, I took guilty pleasure in my solitude, in eating whenever or whatever I wanted, savoring the hours before bedtime, reading a novel or, if I was too tired, mindlessly watching TV.

Maybe I'm unfit for anyone's company but my own, I told Ellen then.

Don't be ridiculous.

I mean it. I miss Joe, but I don't miss having to—it's hard to explain— negotiate *over everything.*

She laughed. *I know what you mean. But Hank and I don't do that much anymore. I have my sphere of influence, he has his. We've worked it out.*

You're a nicer person than I am.

I'm just realistic. Two people can't occupy the same space without a lot of compromise. But if you find the right person, you can work it out.

But until Tony, I've never come close to cohabitation again. There was the sexy carpenter who built new cabinets for the condo. *I'll just leave my tools here until the job's finished,* he said. He'd pick up something for dinner and have it waiting for me when I got home from the office. He had a nice muscled chest and took pride in his work—both the carpentry and the lovemaking—but when he started hinting about moving in, I panicked. I couldn't imagine living with him for the next year, much less the rest of my life. And by then I had my mother.

"Good heavens!" she says as I come in with the beagle. She only says 'Good heavens' when she's trying to impress someone. Even "Good Lord!" is to be avoided in polite company—like Ed Shand, who's sitting next to her on the sofa, his arm over her shoulder. The living room's dark except for the TV. He jumps to attention, mumbling something about Humphrey Bogart. I flick on the ceiling light. Delores, who's stretched out in Mom's recliner, opens her eyes.

"Sorry I'm running late," I say.

"We've been doing fine here," says Ed. "Your mother just loves *Casablanca*."

"Ed cooked dinner for us," says Mom, patting the beagle's head. "He's such a splendid cook! Don't you agree, Delores?"

"Spending the night?" says Delores, eyeing the dog.

But my mother misunderstands. "Oh, no," she says, blushing. "We aren't—"

"Not that I wouldn't jump at any chance to spend more time with your lovely mother," Ed says to me, "but I should be going. Looks like you have a full house tonight, anyway." He kisses my mother's hand. "Good night, Margaret. Thanks for the advice, Delores. Good night, Sally."

"What advice?" I ask Delores when he's gone.

"I told him he better be careful," she says.

"Good."

"Stop that!" she says to Carmen, who's sniffing her shoes. "You go on, now, get away from me!"

"I'm sorry you had to stay late." I tell her about the missing cat. "But she's okay. Maureen—the vet's receptionist—has her."

"Good. We don't need no cat around here. And not another *dog*, neither."

I'm too tired to argue. "Have a good weekend, Delores. See you Monday."

Before she goes, Delores whispers into my ear, "I told Mr. Ed Shand about your mama's sickness, how her mind's all messed up. I told him he best be careful, 'cause if he breaks her heart, I'm gonna break his skinny little neck."

"You said that?"

"Not those exact words, but he got the message!"

Making the Best of It

———◆———

It takes forever to settle them down, the beagle and Mom. As I help her into the shower she's still prattling on about Ed's antiques, talking loud enough for me to hear her through the rush of water. Carmen won't stop barking until I get Mom out, licks her wet legs until I shoo her away. Mom pulls the towel tighter around her breasts. "Don't let him see me naked!"

"Carmen's a girl," I say, as if that makes any difference. "Let's get you into your nightgown."

"I told your father, maybe we could get a little dog, like a Chihuahua. Now look what he's done! Gone and gotten himself a hunting dog!"

"I don't think Carmen's a hunter."

"It's in his blood, though. You wait. He'll be trouble. But I guess you can keep him if you promise to take care of him." The dog has made herself at home on the end of the bed. "I don't want to clean up after him."

"Carmen's a *she*, Mom, and she's housebroken."

"Before you know it, we'll have a litter of puppies."

"No puppies, Mom. She's been fixed."

"I knew we'd end up with a hunting dog. Your father never listens!"

I won't remind her that her husband's been dead for almost forty years. I read her a chapter of *Travels with Charley*, turn off the bedside lamp, wait in the chair beside the bed until I hear her snoring.

I'm almost asleep when Tony calls back. "Oh, sorry," he says. "I forgot the time difference. What's this about the cat?"

"She wasn't there—at your house, I mean. Maureen left a note, says Beatrice is okay, but I'm worried. You have her cell number?"

"Wait a minute. . . . Here it is. . . . What about the dogs. They okay?"

"The retrievers are fine. Carmen's acting a little strange, like she knows something's wrong."

"You're getting pretty good at reading animal minds, aren't you?"

"She's nervous, and when I started to leave she got really upset, so I brought her home with me. By the way, your friend's car wasn't out front."

"I forgot to tell you," he says. "She decided to give her kid his Christmas present early."

"The whole thing really freaked me out."

"Sorry."

"How's your visit going?"

"Okay, I guess." He doesn't sound convincing.

"He's with you now?"

"In the other room, playing a game on his iPad. We're at a motel. I miss you."

"Did you see the interview?" He hasn't seen it, which is good, because I don't want him to hear this news on CNN. "I might keep Carmen, if that's okay."

"Sure it's okay. . . . It was my idea in the first place, remember? Wait a minute. . . . I'm closing the door. . . . Does this mean we're divorcing?"

"What?"

"You say you're keeping Carmen. I guess that means we're not going to be living together anymore."

"Tony, we *don't* live together."

"But we've been talking about it."

"Talking isn't the same as doing." I'm surprised at how mean I sound. "Sorry, I'm really exhausted."

"I'll let you go, then," he says. "If there's any problem with the cat, Beverly McKee is covering my emergencies."

But the problem with the cat isn't anything a vet can fix. "He said he was from the Probate Court," Maureen explains when I finally reach her. "He showed up at the clinic just before closing. He had a court order. Something about a new guardian."

"Did he give you a copy of the order?"

"No, but he showed it to me. It looked legit," she says.

"So you didn't get a copy?"

"I just didn't think—"

"He has Beatrice?"

"Did I screw up?"

"What about a card? Did he leave a card?"

"No, he seemed like he was in a hurry to pick up the cat. I was getting ready to close up for the afternoon, so I told him, 'You just wait here in the parking lot, I'll go pick her up.' But he said he wanted to follow me over there, save me the trouble of driving back to the clinic."

"He followed you to Tony's house?"

"Right."

"What did he look like?"

"Tall. Heavy—not fat, just, you know, bulky. Dressed nice, in a suit and all. Late forties, early fifties."

"That's all you can remember?"

"He had real thick, black eyebrows," she says.

"Did he give you his name?"

"I didn't pay much attention since he showed me the order. Maybe Johnson, or Jones."

"What did the order say?"

"It said something about granting him permission . . . no, I think it was 'possession' of Beatrice. I'm really sorry if I screwed up."

It's almost midnight. Tomorrow is Saturday. The Probate Court won't be open until Monday. Even if I can find Judge Clarkson's home number, I'm not going to wake him at this hour. And I know what he's going to say: He doesn't know anything about this.

Randall Mackay has the cat. *Real thick, black eyebrows.*

I try to go back to sleep, but my imagination is wide awake:

Maybe Randall is one of those sickos who enjoys torturing animals.

Maybe he's already killed her. Poisoned her. Shot her. He's a hunter. He has guns.

But Beatrice would try to defend herself, wouldn't she? Scratch his eyes out. Bite the hell out of him. Run away, if she could.

Be logical, I tell myself. *If he wanted to kill the cat, he's already had his chance. Beatrice was there when he left the note on Tony's kitchen counter. He didn't even touch her.*

But now he's gone a step further. And what did old Gordon Houck tell me once, that time I sought his advice in a particularly nasty divorce case? *We lawyers pride ourselves on our ability to predict outcomes, but it's dangerous, predicting the behavior of crazy people—whether their insanity is temporary or permanent. That doesn't mean you have to give up on logic, it just means you'd better be prepared to react when logic lets you down.*

The woman answering at the sheriff's office is irritatingly soothing. She's trained to deal with all kinds of emergencies but also skilled at handling nut cases: "Yes, ma'am? A missing cat? He was impersonating an officer of the court? Yes, ma'am, I'm taking this information down. I'll turn it over to the duty officer, but it may be tomorrow before you get a call back."

Carmen follows me to the kitchen, where I make myself a cup of chamomile tea and give her a bowl of food, stuff I have left over from Sherman. She eats some of it, but nervously, as if I'm going to take it away from her. The tea does nothing to calm me, either.

Trust Enforcer

The beagle is a restless bedmate. She migrates from the foot of
the bed, where I feel the rhythm of her diaphragm against my
feet, to the middle, where she burrows under the bedspread, and
then up to the pillow, her nose under my chin. At last she's still, and
I try to fall back to sleep, but it seems no time at all before she's
standing beside the bed, licking my hand.

"Lie down, honey." When I close my eyes, she lets out a sharp
little bark.

"You need to go out?" I put on some jeans and a sweatshirt, slide
my feet into flip-flops. "Okay. I'm coming."

We ride the elevator down to the lobby and she trots to the main
door. Outside I hold the leash while she arches her back in a strip of
grass near the entrance. She hesitates; she's not accustomed to the
leash. My bare toes are freezing. "Go on," I coax her. "It's okay."
Finally she relaxes, accomplishes her task. I remember the notice on
the bulletin board: *Residents are reminded to clean up after their pets. Scoop
your poop!*

I'll have to get a scooper, and I'll have to figure out a way to accommodate Carmen's needs without leaving Mom alone. This morning she's still fast asleep when I get back upstairs, but I've broken the rule I established for Delores and Shenille: *Never leave Mom in the condo alone, even for five minutes.*

"Better be glad you're my best friend," says Ellen when I call to tell her about the missing cat. "You know it's not even seven yet?"

"I was hoping you might have Judge Clarkson's home number. It's not listed."

"Why would I have his home number?"

"I don't know. I guess I'm not thinking straight."

"Why don't you try Joe? He might have it, or maybe he can get it."

"This isn't Joe's problem."

"He wouldn't mind making a call or two to help you out," she says, "if you really think this is an emergency."

"I need someone to send a deputy out there."

"Out where?"

"Randall Mackay's house. On Edisto Beach."

"Well, that complicates it. Most of the Edisto Island is in Charleston County, but there was some weird political thing, and the beach is actually in Colleton County, so our sheriff doesn't have jurisdiction there."

"But if I have an order from our Probate Court, won't they enforce it?"

"I'm telling you, if you want a deputy to get involved, you're better off going through a judge; otherwise you'll get mired down in interdepartmental bullshit. Wait a minute! What about that woman who lives out there . . . the caretaker for the old lady. She knows Randall, right? Maybe she could help you out."

"I thought about that, but I don't want to get her involved. He's too unpredictable. At this point, I need a judge."

"So, call Joe."

I'm not prepared for Joe's wife to answer his cell phone, so what I say sounds dumb: "Oh, hi, Susan. This is Sally. Sally Baynard. I'm trying to get in touch with Joe."

"He just got out of the shower."

"I hope I didn't wake you."

"Oh, no. I've already finished my morning run."

"It's about Judge Clarkson," I say, feeling the need to explain myself.

"So sad, isn't it?" she says.

"What?"

"That he just keeled over like that, a couple of weeks before his retirement."

"When did—"

"Oh, I assumed you'd heard. Yesterday afternoon, in his office. At least it was mercifully quick."

"That's awful."

"Poor Julia, she really depended on him. She's been so ill. . . . Listen, I'll have Joe call you back. I know he wants to talk to you about something. He has your cell number?"

"Yes."

"Nice to talk to you," she says. "And Sally . . . this is a little awkward, but I want to tell you . . . Joe and I are doing just *fine*." She reminds me of my mother, the way she states something in that chirpy, lilting voice, full of charm and confidence, as if just saying it will make it true.

"I'm glad," I say. "I really am."

. . .

An hour later Joe picks me up in front of my office, where I've gone to get up my copy of the order appointing me as trust enforcer. He's driving a shiny new Mercedes, dark blue. "You didn't have to do this," I say.

He eyes the beagle. "You lose a cat and gain a dog?"

Carmen balks when I open the back door. "Come on, honey, get in."

"No point in resisting, Carmen," Joe says. "If Sally Baynard wants you to do something, you might as well give up and do it." The dog won't budge. I lift her up, put her on the backseat. "I guess this is the one you were talking about on CNN?"

"Oh, you saw that?"

"Me and the rest of the country."

It's strange to sit in the car beside him as we turn the corner onto Lockwood. "If I'd known you had a new car, I'd have brought a towel. She sheds a little."

"Don't worry about it. So, you're going to keep her?"

"I guess so."

"What do you mean, you *guess* so? Now that you've announced it all over the country, you can't exactly give her back, can you?" He smiles. "Especially when you're advertising yourself as animal lawyer extraordinaire!"

"That was Gina's fault. Anyway, thanks for doing this. I just wanted some help getting a deputy—"

"I know Randall. He'll just weasel his way around a deputy, but he's not likely to try any nonsense with me." Joe adjusts his sunglasses. "This cat client of yours sure is a lot of trouble. Black cat, bad luck, right? Poor old Judge Clarkson, maybe she put a curse on him or something."

"That's not funny."

"He didn't get to enjoy even one day of retirement," Joe says. "Tough situation for his wife. She's bedridden. He was totally devoted to her."

"That's what I heard."

"They were one of those special couples. You just couldn't imagine one without the other." Only someone who knows Joe well would notice the change in his voice, the way he clears his throat, straightens his back. "So now, counselor, tell me why you think Randall Mackay is the perpetrator." He listens to the evidence, nods. "I hope we're not too late."

"He just wants to use Beatrice as a bargaining chip."

"As usual, you sound pretty sure of yourself. But let's review the case, Ms. Baynard. One: Randall abuses his first wife. Two: His second wife mysteriously disappears. Three, he steals money from his mother. Four: He's furious because you're taking his mother's wishes seriously, doing your best to enforce the trust. Then he sneaks out to your boyfriend's house in the middle of the night and leaves a threatening note on your windshield."

"I can't prove he did that, not without a handwriting expert."

"You really *are* in denial, aren't you? And now some guy who just happens to fit the description of Randall Mackay shows up at the vet's office, flashes some piece of paper in front of the receptionist, and runs off with the cat—the very same cat who's the beneficiary of a multimillion dollar estate and a plantation, the plantation Randall thinks he's entitled to, which under the terms of the trust, he can't have until the cat dies. You know anyone else who has a motive to off the cat?"

"He's holding her ransom so he can make a deal. He threatened to challenge his mother's competency unless we could reach an agreement that he can have the plantation now."

"But the old lady wanted the cat to live there. So how would that work?"

"Mrs. Mackay named three people as potential caregivers. One of them lives on Edisto. She loves the cat, and the cat seems comfortable with her, but she doesn't want to live in that big house. Randall knows her, and he agrees that she'd make a fine caregiver, but he says, why not let the cat live with Gail in her trailer? It's not so unreasonable. A cat doesn't need a plantation."

"Except that's not what Mrs. Mackay specified in the trust, and you have a duty to carry out the testator's wishes, if possible," Joe says.

"But it seems to me that the most important thing is Beatrice's welfare. She'll be perfectly fine living in a trailer, as long as she's loved and cared for," I say, trying to convince myself. "I've interviewed the other two candidates. The nephew won't leave New York. The librarian would be willing to move to Edisto, but she's married, and I don't trust her husband."

"This might be a purely theoretical discussion if the cat's already gone to feline heaven. Anyway, it's a nice drive. How's your mother, by the way?"

"She's got a boyfriend. An old friend from Columbia who just happened to move into the building."

"I hope you didn't leave them unchaperoned." He laughs.

"I called the weekend sitter."

"It's nice that she's got some love in her life," he says.

"She could get hurt. I don't think this guy has any idea what he's gotten himself into."

Randall Mackay's house is one of the original oceanfront places, two stories with a cupola at the top, wraparound porches. It's been updated, probably added onto over the years. There's some expensive landscaping on the street side: palm trees, a fountain.

"You stay here," says Joe. I watch him go up the steps and open the screen door. Then I lose sight of him.

This was a bad idea, I think. *If he's not back in five minutes I'm going to call 911.*

But he doesn't take that long. When he comes back, he shakes his head. "Nobody home. I nosed around the garage just to make sure. No cars in there. Guess you'll have to wait until Monday, see if you can get the assistant probate judge to authorize an all-points bulletin."

"I feel like I've really let her down."

"Let who down?"

"The cat. I should never have left her at Tony's."

I can see him flinch at the sound of the name. "Let's not get into that, okay? While we're out here, we might as well have some lunch. I hear the marina restaurant's pretty good."

"But what about Carmen?" The beagle, who's been sleeping, lifts her ears. "I can't leave her in the car."

"We can pick up something on the way back, then."

"I'm really sorry you had to drive all the way out here for nothing," I say.

"I wanted to talk to you anyway, about the Circuit Court judgeship," he says. "I need your help."

"Joe, you know I'm no good at politics."

"If I want this, I'll have to fight for it."

"You sound like you're not so sure."

"I have to do it, otherwise I'm just sitting around in the Family Court until I retire. And Susan insists. It's the next step."

"Joe!" I'm yelling, and Carmen's barking. "This is your *life* we're talking about!"

"Shut that dog up, would you?"

"Come on," I say to Carmen, and coax her through the space between the seats and onto my lap. "You could always go back to practicing law."

"I don't have what it takes anymore."

"My point is, you don't decide you want a circuit judgeship because you're just putting one foot in front of the other." As I say this, I'm suddenly thrown back to our old arguments. I'd criticize the way he seemed to follow the path his father and his grandfather had chosen for him; he'd defend his choices.

"I'm not asking for a lecture," he says. "I just want to make sure, if I go for this judgeship, that you won't say anything that would hurt me."

"Of course I won't."

"It's just that with the divorce, there might be some questions."

"You certainly won't be the first judicial candidate who's divorced. And you aren't a drunkard, a drug abuser, or a wife-beater."

"That's not exactly an enthusiastic endorsement," he says.

"If anyone asks, which they won't, I'll say we were just too young, we were incompatible, and it was my decision to leave. That's the truth, isn't it? And of course nobody's going to question your qualifications."

"The word is, Cynthia Halleck is interested."

"She's too young, don't you think?"

"Maybe, but she's been practicing in Circuit Court for ten years, and meanwhile I've been stuck in the Family Court."

"But you've got judicial experience."

"Wayne Murrell's pushing her. All of a sudden he's a feminist. And he's got his coterie of plaintiff's lawyers up there in the legislature."

"You've got plenty of connections yourself, Joe."

"That's why I was hoping you could help me line up some support among the women lawyers before Cynthia has them all in her corner."

"I don't know, Joe." Now it's clear to me why he was so accommodating about driving me to Edisto. "I'll have to think about it. I've never gotten involved in a judicial race."

"It was actually Susan's idea. Maybe she thinks you owe it to her."

I can feel the blood surging to my cheeks. "I haven't done anything to Susan."

"I know that, but she doesn't." We're quiet the rest of the way back to the city. Just before he drops me off in front of my building, he touches the top of my hand. "So, you'll let me know soon? Don't let that dog get away from you, okay? It might ruin your reputation!"

He's trying to be funny, but I'd like to slap him.

A Spot of Blood

Y ou look like hell," says Gina on Monday morning. She's brought the mail and a cup of coffee for me, which is always her invitation to talk. The beagle comes out from under my desk to greet her. "Who's this?"

"Carmen."

"Oh, this the one from Dr. Borden? You going to keep her?" I nod. "She's a cutie. So, guess she must have kept you awake last night?"

"I can't blame it on her. I had a terrible weekend." I tell her about the missing cat, Judge Clarkson, the trip out to Edisto Beach.

"You sure he's got her? Randall, I mean."

"Pretty sure."

"My weekend wasn't so great, either. But we don't have to talk about it now." I can see she's on the verge of tears. Before I know it, we're sitting together on my sofa and I'm handing her a tissue. "I broke things off with Rick." The tears I've been holding back come pouring out. We cry until Carmen begins to howl in sympathy, and then we laugh.

"He was pretty mad," she says between sobs, "but I just didn't feel good about the way things were going. And he was actually getting jealous of Mandy."

"Ellen's Mandy?"

"She's a great kid. I've been talking to her about how she can make it work—you know, with the baby."

"She likes you a lot."

"I just don't want to see her give up the college thing, like I did. She could go part-time."

"Maybe."

"I've got an extra bedroom at my place."

"That's a lot for you to take on, Gina."

"Hey, you didn't ask my permission when *you* got a new room-mate!" She pats Carmen's head.

When we've stopped crying, she points to the stack of mail on my desk. "There's one I didn't open, because it's marked *Personal and Confidential.*"

There's no return address. I slide my index finger under the flap, feel a sting when I rip it open too fast, and before I know it there's a spot of blood on the letter. "Ouch!" I say. The beagle whimpers.

"You should use the letter opener," says Gina.

The letter's typed, undated:

My Dear Trust Enforcer,
> *You're aren't taking very good care of me, are you?*
> *Surely Gail could do a better job. Let's settle this case.*
> *Trusting in your better judgment,*
> *Beatrice*

My hands are shaking.

"It's Randall, isn't it?" Gina says. "What are we going to do?"

"Let's play his game. Call him—his number's in the file—and

tell him I received his letter and would like to talk to him. If he asks any questions, just say you don't know anything more. And take notes, in case you have to testify later."

"Should I tell him to bring the cat?"

"Just say I received the letter and want to talk to him."

"The guy's probably deranged, and you want to invite him to our office?"

"It's a long shot, but I think it might work."

"*What* might work?"

"I'll explain it later. I've got the Farrell adoption at ten." The truth is, I'm not sure what I'm going to say to Randall Mackay, if he comes.

She hands me the file. "By the way, I found that old man . . . the one who used to own the bookstore. He lives on Gadsden Street. I'll leave the info on your desk. I told him you'd be calling, but he's a little deaf, so maybe it would be better for you to talk to him in person."

The waiting room at Family Court is filled with the aggrieved, the vengeful, the punitive plaintiffs versus the desperate defendants, and those who've resigned themselves to love's limitless capacity to disappoint. Whether they win or lose, they'll soon be as unhappy as they were when they came into the courtroom. I don't recognize these faces, but I can imagine their stories. That woman there, clutching her pocketbook, may prevail in the custody battle for her kids, and she'll get a piece of paper requiring her husband to pay child support, but on the bus ride home she'll figure out that after she pays her rent, she won't have much left over. The fellow next to her—the one with the trim goatee and the cashmere sports jacket—may escape his two-year marriage without financial obligations, but he'll wonder, as he drives his Saab out of the parking garage, why he doesn't feel like celebrating.

I've spent two decades as a lawyer in this court, and though I've won more cases than I've lost, I've rarely felt victorious. Sure, it's gratifying to hear a judge rule in my client's favor, but in your average divorce there's not enough money to go around, and even when there's plenty, the divvying-up is a depressing business.

I've been here myself as a plaintiff, in the case of *Sarah Bright Baynard vs. Joseph Henry Baynard*. I had no illusions. I didn't come to court imagining that a divorce would be my ticket to happiness. I wanted it to be the official end to our struggle, so that we could quit our squabbling and blaming, but I've never felt more bereft than when the clerk handed me my certified copy of the Final Order and Decree of Divorce. There was nothing final about it at all.

This morning I have the rare experience of representing happy people. I spot them in the far corner of the waiting area, Allison and Tom Farrell, both in their mid-forties, a couple who'd given up on children until I got a call from an old law school acquaintance who remembered I handle adoptions. The daughter of one his one of his clients was six months pregnant, wanted to find a good home for her baby.

Almost twenty years ago I represented Tom Farrell in a juvenile case. He'd taken his uncle's car for a joyride and wrecked it. Tom was sixteen, but the uncle was unforgiving. I can still remember how his whole body shook as I stood next to him in the courtroom, my arm around his shoulder. The judge gave him a lengthy lecture and probation. He stayed out of trouble after that. Now he's got a good job at Boeing and he's been married to Allison for ten years. Baby Suzannah is in her lap.

"We'll never be able to thank you enough for this," says Tom, who carries the diaper bag and the foldable stroller. "It's the best day of our lives!" This has been a long time coming. I'd found a baby for them a couple of years ago, but the birth mother changed her mind once she saw her newborn daughter.

"Who's the judge?" asks Allison.

"Beverly O'Neill. She has two adopted kids herself."

"She won't give me any trouble about the juvenile thing, will she?" asks Tom.

"The guardian *ad litem*'s not concerned about that at all. She thinks you hung the moon." But where is she? Martha Query should be here already. "And Judge O'Neill's very easygoing."

But when we walk into the courtroom the judge behind the bench is Joe Baynard. I whisper into Tom's ear, "They've switched judges on us, but it doesn't matter."

"Good morning, Your Honor," I begin. "We're ready to proceed, except for the guardian *ad litem*. I'm sure she's on her way, if Your Honor would—"

"If she can be here in five minutes, we'll proceed."

I search the file for Martha's number. It should be on the inside of the folder along with the Farrells' phone numbers and addresses. "I'm looking for her number, Your Honor." Could Gina have forgotten to notify her of the hearing?

"I suggest you try Information, Ms. Baynard. That is, if you haven't lost your cell phone, too."

"Yes, sir."

"It isn't like you to be disorganized, Ms. Baynard," says Joe. "But this is such a nice-looking family, I won't hold you in contempt!" It's the kind of joke that isn't funny to nervous clients. He addresses the next comment to them: "As I'm sure you're aware, your attorney is highly respected in the Charleston bar, and now she's developing a national reputation. Let's hope the sudden fame hasn't gone to her head!" Why is he acting like this? Is he angry because I wouldn't commit to help him with his judicial race?

Tom Farrell sweats in his too-tight suit. Allison does her best to calm the squirming baby. Just then the guardian *ad litem* walks in, breathless. "I'm so sorry, Your Honor. I got stuck in traffic."

After the hearing, I wait for the clerk to certify the adoption order so that I can present a copy to the Farrells. They're ecstatic.

"We'll never be able to thank you enough," says Allison. "Here, you hold her for a minute so I can take a picture. When she's old enough, we can tell her all about you."

The baby feels incredibly light, as if she's going to fly out of my hands. She opens her eyes, stares up at me with unfocused wonderment.

"There," says Allison. "I think I got a couple of good ones."

"Let me take one of you and Tom and the baby," I offer.

"Isn't it amazing?" says Allison. "She's really ours. I just want us to be worthy of her."

"Is that judge related to you?" asks Tom.

I could lie, but why bother? "He's my ex-husband. We were married briefly, a long time ago."

"Maybe I shouldn't say it," says Allison, "but he seems like kind of a jerk."

I nod. Why do I feel guilty about not defending him?

"But nothing can spoil this day for us," says Tom. "She's an angel, isn't she?"

A Preponderance of the Evidence

————✦————

Back at the office, I try to concentrate on Gina's draft of the inter-
rogatories in the Carter case. No matter how well they're crafted,
how careful we are in asking these questions, Derwood will do his
best to evade a truthful answer. He'll object to some of them as
"overly broad," to others as "repetitive." He's trying to intimidate
me with his premature request for a trial date, but he can't have it
both ways: If he wants a quick trial, he'll have to cooperate with
discovery.

But I can't concentrate. I keep thinking about Beatrice, wonder-
ing what advice old Judge Clarkson would have given me. I can see
him leaning back in his chair, rubbing his belly as he considers the
problem. *The cat's been missing for two days now. If she were a child, and you
were her guardian, what would you do?*

Carmen's as restless as I am. "Lie down," I say, a little too sternly,
and then, "I'm sorry. It's not *your* fault."

I call the Probate Court to schedule a conference with Judge Wilson. "Yes, it's an emergency," I explain. "She's swamped, as you can
imagine," says her secretary, "but I'll see if we can't work you in sometime later this week, okay?"

I call Ellen. I need her steady voice, her reassurance. She's in trial, says the receptionist, so I leave a message. My head is starting to pound, my mind spinning in a labyrinth of horrors: Turn here, a cat starving in Randall's basement. There, my mother and Ed Shand, contorted like the couples I saw in those photos I stole so long ago.

I close my eyes, feel something rest against my thigh, a warm weight. It's the beagle. I stroke her forehead. "Don't worry," I say, "everything will be okay." She looks up at me as if she believes me.

"Randall Mackay is coming at two," says Gina.

"Did he say anything about Beatrice?"

"He was pretty cagey. He said . . . Wait a minute, I wrote it down: 'I'm glad your boss is finally coming to her senses.' You think he's crazy enough to hurt her?"

"He can't use a dead cat as a bargaining chip."

"If he killed her, it doesn't seem right that he'd get the plantation."

And then it comes to me, the memory from law school: the overheated classroom, the fat textbook open in front of me, the professor droning on and on. The course in Trusts and Estates, which I'd taken only because it was required for graduation. I'm sitting in the back row, trying to stay awake, when he surprises me with his question: *And what if there are two beneficiaries, and one kills the other? Can the surviving beneficiary claim the deceased's share?* I snap awake: *No, sir.* My answer is a gut reaction, but of course he wants more, and I can't remember the relevant case law. I stammer as he moves on to another student.

It wasn't like me to be unprepared for class. My excuse wasn't one I could share: I'd been up all night with one Joseph Henry Baynard, the fellow student sitting next to me. We'd started the evening with good intentions, determined to study, but we took a break for a beer and soon found ourselves less interested in Trusts and Estates than in each other.

"You're right: If he kills the cat," I explain to Gina, "he can't profit from his wrongdoing. Wait a minute. . . ." I log on to the South Carolina Bar website, type the words "homicide beneficiary wills" into the search bar. "Here it is—they've codified the old case law, expanded on it. Section 62-2-803: *Effect of homicide on intestate succession, wills, joint assets, life insurance, and beneficiary designations.*"

"So," says Gina,"the bottom line is that if he kills the cat, he can't get what he wants—which is the plantation. You think he knows that?"

"I doubt it, but we'll educate him."

He smiles like a man who's sure he's already won, his tongue sweeping his bottom lip as if he's tasting his victory. "Well, I'm glad you finally came to your senses," he says. I'm two feet away, but I can smell the alcohol on his breath.

"I have indeed," I say, opening the volume of the Code to the place I've marked. I seldom use these books anymore, but today I need what old Judge Clarkson would call their "heft."

"You don't need a law book to settle this thing." He stands on the other side of my desk, a massive man, his chest and shoulders straining the seams of his sports coat. "And you don't need a guard dog, either." He glares at Carmen, who's growling. "Shut up, you runt."

"Please sit down," I say.

"Okay, okay. Don't want to make anybody nervous."

"Are you intoxicated?"

"Nah."

"Good, because I want you to understand what I'm about to say."

"You'd better say I'm going to get what I'm entitled to."

"Mr. Mackay, what you're entitled to is what your mother left you, by way of a legal document that's enforceable under South Carolina law."

"Not if the old bitch was out of her mind."

"Based on what I've learned about you, I think it's amazing your mother left you anything at all. I'm not your lawyer, but if you hire one, she'll explain that you can contest the trust if you choose to, but if you lose, you'll forfeit your right to the remainder."

"I'm not here for a lecture," he says, still holding on to the desk.

"You need to return Beatrice to me by five P.M. this afternoon."

"That's what you made me come here for, just to tell me that?"

"You're in a bind, Mr. Mackay. If anything happens to the cat, this law"—I pat the Code as if it's my best buddy—"says that you don't get a thing. I'll be happy to make you a copy, but let me read it to you: 'An individual who feloniously and intentionally kills the decedent is not entitled to any benefit under the decedent's will or trust . . . and the estate of the decedent passes as if the killer had predeceased the decedent.' Now, of course, the decedent is your mother, and you didn't kill her, she died in the hospital."

"Right, so you're wasting your breath."

"But the statute further provides . . . Let me read you the exact words: 'A beneficiary whose interest is increased as a result of feloniously and intentionally killing shall be treated in accordance with the principles of this section.' That means that if you kill Beatrice, you can't get the property any earlier than you would have had she lived, and I will take the position that the statute precludes you from *ever* getting it." I close the book. "As I said, I'll be happy to make you a copy."

"I never said I had the damn cat," he growls. "If something's happened to her, you can't prove I had anything to do with it. Cats disappear all the time."

"I'm not going to outline my case for you, Mr. Mackay, but suffice it to say that I have more than sufficient evidence to prove you took her. And the statute I just referred to helps me in that regard. You're familiar with the standard of proof in criminal cases— 'beyond a reasonable doubt'?" He doesn't answer, just glares. "That standard is a difficult one to satisfy, but in this case I won't have to worry about it, because this statute gives me a break. It says that I only have to prove my case by a 'preponderance of the evidence.' That's a lot easier."

He stands up, "You tricked me into coming here. You don't want to talk settlement."

"I wouldn't talk settlement with you unless I was worried about losing. But *you're* the one who's going to lose if Beatrice isn't safely in my office by five P.M. this afternoon. And let me say one thing further: If someone else is holding her for you, you're taking a big chance, because if anything happens to her, I'll take the position that she died as a result of your recklessness. Do you understand that?"

He looks at his watch. "You're not giving me much time."

"It's plenty of time for you to produce the cat, unless she's dead."

He turns to leave. "She was a terrible mother." His voice is almost inaudible.

"Excuse me?"

"Lila Mackay was a terrible mother."

"It's not my job to defend your mother. My job is to protect the cat, to choose the best caregiver for her, to make sure, as best I can, that your mother's wishes with regard to Beatrice are carried out."

As he's leaving he mutters, "Maybe you won't believe it, but when I was little, I really loved her."

. . .

Just before five o'clock, Ellen returns my call. "Sorry," she says.
"I was in trial. Horrible murder case. I feel like I need to stand
under a shower for a couple of hours, just to wash the blood away.
What's up?"

"I needed a pep talk, but I think I've got it under control now. . . .
I'll know in another five minutes."

"Want to get a drink? I could sure use one."

"I have the new dog with me. And maybe the cat."

"Tell you what, why don't I grab a bottle of wine and something
for dinner and come over to your place? Hank won't be home till
late. He's meeting with some people about sharing office space."

"I'll have my mother, and maybe Delores. Sometimes she stays
for dinner."

"I'll bring enough for everybody."

Gina, Carmen, and I wait in the reception area. Gina and I watch
the clock: 4:50, 4:51 . . . 4:57. Carmen lies on the floor, gnawing at a
spot on her hip. "She's going to rub that place raw," says Gina. "You
should get the vet to look at it. . . . How's that going, anyway?"

Before I can say I don't really want to talk about it, we hear the
hum of the elevator as it rises to our floor, the thump as it jerks to a
stop, and the door opening with its usual deep wheeze. We wait for
the sound of footsteps in the hall, but nothing. The door closes, and
Gina shakes her head.

Then there's a "meow," and another—louder, insistent, as if Beatrice is saying, *I'm right here. Are you going to leave me here all night?* We
rush into the hall. I lift her out of her carrier, stroke her. She seems
fine, as fat as ever, but she's not interested in me. She wants the new
toy—a fake mouse that squeaks when she bats it around, a toy that
Randall must have given her.

Who Am I Saving It For?

S he's been real upset this afternoon," says Delores when I get home. She frowns at the beagle and the cat, this time with more resignation than resistance. "I just got her settled down. She's watching a Denzel movie." My mother adores Denzel. *He's so intelligent,* she said not long ago, *such a credit to his people!* I used to confront her about statements like this, but Delores convinced me to let them go. *She is who she is. Don't you worry, we get along fine.*

"What got her upset?" I ask.

"She kept saying Mr. Shand had a heart attack. Wanted to go visit him in the hospital."

"It was my dad who had the heart attack."

"He was here this morning—Mr. Shand—said he had to go to the doctor, so maybe that's what got her started."

"I wish he'd leave her alone."

"Nobody's going to keep those two apart," Delores says with finality, "Not unless you want to move to another building—maybe another country! There's no harm in it. He behaves himself." She turns toward the cat, who's exploring some plastic containers on the kitchen counter. "You scat now, get out of my kitchen!"

"Ellen's coming over, bringing some dinner. You're welcome to stay."

"I have choir practice."

"You joined the choir?" Delores has a gorgeous voice, but I've heard it only when she's singing to herself in the kitchen. "I thought you didn't like to perform in public."

"People tell me I got this gift, and I started thinking, *Who am I saving it for?* I used to sing for Charlie. He was always after me to join the choir, so . . . I just figured it was time. You got to take the gifts God gives you, make the most of them."

"Charlie was a wise man."

"Speaking of gifts, what about you and that vet?"

"It's complicated."

"Well, like I told you, anything to do with a man and a woman's gonna be complicated, but—"

"You're the one who wouldn't move in with Charlie until he was dying!" I'm not in the mood for a lecture from Delores.

She gets her purse, pulls her coat over her shoulders. She won't even look at me.

"I'm sorry. I shouldn't have said that."

"When you learn how to love a man like I loved Charlie, you let me know, okay?" She closes the door hard on her way out.

By the time Ellen comes with a bottle of wine and takeout from Tasty Thai, I've fed the animals, changed into jeans and a sweatshirt, given Mom a shower, and gotten her into a nightgown. "Not *that*!" she said when I handed her the flannel one Delores had left on the end of the bed. I was too tired for a battle, so I gave in. She chose the pink satiny one, which seems too nice to sleep in, more like an evening gown, and the matching bathrobe and slippers. And then she insisted on earrings and perfume.

"You want a glass of wine, Margaret?" asks Ellen. "It's a nice Pinot Grigio."

"She shouldn't," I say. "Not with her medication."

"Half a glass won't hurt anything, will it, Margaret?" says Ellen.

Mom smiles, and I give in. She's already helping herself to the Pad Thai. "Let me get your bib, Mom," I say. "You don't want to ruin that robe. Wasn't Ellen nice to bring all this?"

"Happy to do it," says Ellen.

"It's been crazy, these last couple of days." I fill her in on the trip to Edisto with Joe, the meeting with Randall Mackay.

"At least you got the cat back," she says. Beatrice is under the table, rubbing the back of my legs. "What are you going to do about him? . . . Joe, I mean."

Mom perks up at the sound of his name, wipes a noodle off her chin with the sleeve of her robe. "Joe says I'm the most beautiful mother-in-law he ever had."

"It's true, Margaret," says Ellen, "you *are* beautiful. "

"I have my hair done every Wednesday," says Mom. Before my mother sank into her dementia, she gave me strict instructions for her funeral: Episcopal, of course, no open coffin, but a fresh hairdo by her regular hairdresser.

What does it matter what your hair looks like, I said, *if you're not going to have an open coffin?*

She looked at me, did one of her quick inspections for defects, and said, *If you took any pride in your appearance, you'd understand why it matters.*

"Your hair always looks perfect," Ellen says to Mom. And to me: "So, are you going to help him with the campaign?"

"I don't know." The beagle, who's been hanging around the table, not exactly begging but vigilant in case something falls to the floor, settles herself on the mat below the sink. "I'd like to help him out, but Cynthia's certainly qualified, and we worked together on the women's shelter board."

"Has she asked you to back her?"

"No, I didn't know a thing about it until Joe mentioned her."

"The easiest thing would be to just stay out of it," she says.

"But what do I tell him?"

"Tell him the truth, that it's just too uncomfortable for you." She bites into a spring roll.

"I'm trying to be objective. He's got loads of judicial experience, and except for the dog case, I don't know of anything—"

"I'm going to be brutally frank," says Ellen. "Whenever you talk about him, I feel like there's still something—"

"I just don't want to hurt him . . . with his campaign, I mean."

"Think about it. You've never gotten involved in judicial politics, so why start now?"

"Because he's asked for my support."

"Did Susan know he was chauffeuring you to Edisto?"

"I think it was her idea. She's more ambitious than he is!"

Ellen frowns. "I'm telling you, you're asking for trouble if you get involved. Margaret, would you like some more?" My mother nods. Her appetite is still good.

"But enough about me," I say. "How's Mandy?"

And of course it's her daughter she really wants to talk about: the girl who until a month ago was headed for Duke on full scholarship. "She says it's all going to work out," Ellen says with a sigh, "because she's moving in with Gina, and Gina was a single parent herself, and Gina loves children. All I've heard out of her mouth for the past couple of days is Gina, Gina, Gina. If I didn't *like* Gina, I'd want to kill her. This wasn't your idea, was it?"

"Of course not. I've been pushing—gently—for adoption."

My mother perks up: "You never know what you're going to get with an adopted child. It's potluck!"

"Hank wants her to stay with us at least until the baby's born," says Ellen, "but she's determined to be on her own."

"Well, you brought her up to be independent."

"But she's ruining her life. . . . Dammit, I didn't come over here to cry."

"Sometimes you just need to cry your heart out," says my mother. "It helps to run a hot bath, darling, and then you can cry all you want to. You'll feel better once you get it all out." She's never said anything this comforting to me. It was always: *Stand up straight, put a smile on your face, quit feeling sorry for yourself.*

"Maybe I'll do that when I get home," says Ellen.

We clean up, I put Mom to bed, make a pot of coffee, sit up with Ellen for a while longer. Beatrice is curled in my lap. "That cat looks right at home," she says.

"She's not staying, if that's what you're thinking."

"So who are you going to give her to?"

"I've almost made up my mind. I have a couple of people I still want to talk to. You remember Mr. Witowski, who owned the bookstore on King Street?"

"I thought he was dead. How'd you come up with *him*?"

"Long story."

"But he wasn't on the list."

"No, it's more out of curiosity than anything else."

"God, I miss that bookstore. Remember the cats?"

Old Books and Candle Wax

———◆———

Simon Witowski's apartment is on the second floor, reachable only by a set of outside stairs that run from the lower piazza to the one above. The railings are rickety, a couple of the balusters missing. The house—antebellum, once a single-family dwelling—badly needs painting. It stands out among the others on Gadsden Street, all of which have been redone in pastel colors approved by the Board of Architectural Review.

"I'm in the process of moving, so things are a little chaotic," he'd said when I called to confirm the appointment. When I step inside I see what he means: There are piles of books on the floor, on the dining room table, on every available surface. He points to the cardboard boxes under the table. "Would you like a cup of tea?"

He's thin, his gray wool jacket too big for him, the excess fabric of the trousers bunched into his belt, but despite an obvious limp there's a surprising vitality about him. "I had a little accident a few years back, tripped—ankle's never been quite the same. . . . Yes, I remember you from the bookstore. You were quite keen on short stories, weren't you? Flannery O'Connor, Mary Gordon."

"You introduced me to Lorrie Moore."

"Ah, yes. *Birds of America*! Milk, sugar?"

"No, this is fine, thank you."

"The new owners couldn't keep up with the rent increases," he says. "King Street's gone very posh, you know. And even Gadsden Street now . . . This neighborhood used to be a melting pot, a little bit of this, a little bit of that—medical students, faculty from the college, young couples just starting out, the older ones like me—but everything's changed. Some people from New Jersey just bought this one. Oh, watch your step there," he says, pointing to a litter box. "I've been meaning to get rid of that."

"You have a cat?"

"It's left over from McCavity. You might remember him from the bookstore."

"The big yellow one?"

"Old devil finally passed away. About a month ago."

"I'm sorry."

"He was the last of my bookstore cats. But when you're as old as I am, you accustom yourself to losses."

"When are you moving?"

"I must be out by January first. I'll have a small room at the Franke Home, so most of these books are going to the county library for their fund-raising sale. You're welcome to look through them before you go."

He catches my expression as I survey the room. "Yes, I know, I haven't made much progress."

"Do you have some help with all this?"

"My niece wants me to hire a crew, but I can't tolerate strangers handling my books. And there's the expense."

The whole place smells like old books and candle wax. There's a menorah on a little table in the corner, and beside it a potted plant hung with Christmas ornaments. "That's for my great-nephews," he explains. "My niece married, as my mother would have said, out of the tribe. She brings her boys around on Christmas afternoon, so I do my best to be ecumenical. It's just a small party, my family and a few others. But you came to talk about the cat, isn't that right?"

"As I told you, my job is to choose a caregiver for her."

"I haven't met Beatrice," he says. "But I understand she's highly intelligent and rather temperamental, like her owner. I remember when Lila named her. I assumed some reference to Dante's beloved, so I joked to Lila that if she ever felt lost in purgatory, the cat might lead her out. She took offense." He smiles. "She could be quite thin-skinned. . . . Who's keeping the cat now?"

"She's staying with me until I've finished my investigation. Mrs. Mackay named three people as possible caregivers."

"Yes, you told me."

"Your name wasn't on the list, yet she kept some of your letters, and I . . . I can't help but think she did so for a reason, that maybe she intended you to shed some light on——"

"Or perhaps she was merely sentimental," he says.

"I was told by her nephew Philip that you and Mrs. Mackay were very close at one time."

"Philip—how is he these days?"

"He seems well."

"What a talent! I do hope he's still writing. I haven't had a letter from him in a while, but then of course no one writes letters any-more, and I don't do e-mail."

"He shared some of your story with me . . . your relationship with Lila."

"Philip was one of the few people she told about it, but even Philip didn't know everything," he says.

"If you wouldn't mind, I'd like to hear it."

"I suppose there's no harm, now that she's gone, though I doubt our story will shed any light on your task. A little more tea?"

Simon and Lila

———✦———

My father was a fine tailor, much in demand. His parents had left Russia around the turn of the century, because of the pogroms. They were old-world Jews, very insular, and although he was born in Charleston, he seldom ventured outside the circle of his family. He worked very hard, paid for the building on King Street over a period of thirty years, and of course he expected me—his only son—to take over the business. But my mother was more imaginative, and her family was a little more sophisticated. She had a brother in New York who ran a bookstore on the Upper East Side. She sent me up there one summer to, as she said, "polish me up a little." My uncle put me to work in his store. I adored it: the store, the neighborhood, the city. At the end of the summer I came home, not happily, for my senior year in high school. In the afternoons, after school I helped my father in his shop. I could see my future laid out before me—an eternity of measuring tapes and inseams.

But if it hadn't been for that shop I would never have met Lila. We had closed for the day; my father had gone home and I was sweeping up. She ignored the "closed" sign, knocked on the door. I could see her through the glass, that imperious, exasperated expression: How dare we close the store! *I let her in, found her father's trousers, and took her money. She was pretty. Bright-*

eyed, intelligent, and though I knew better—she was one of those Ashley Hall girls, definitely out of my league—I was smitten.

She was headed up north for college. Vassar. The moment I heard this, I turned my back on the College of Charleston and devised a way to go back to New York. I got a scholarship to City College, roomed with my cousin and his wife. Lila would come down to the city on weekends and we . . . well, I had a classmate who had his own apartment on Houston Street, and he'd lend it to us for an hour or two at a time. Our times there were glorious. This went on for several years. I was so naive.

And then I received a letter from her announcing her engagement. She said she was sorry, but she'd known for a while it would never work out—we were just too "different." She would always love me, she wrote, and she hoped we'd stay in touch. I didn't write back. She moved back to Charleston and I stayed on in New York.

I didn't see her for years. She sent some breezy letters, photos of Oak Bluff. She'd always felt a strong attachment to the place. Not just the house, which— oh, you've been there?—is nothing grand compared to some of the others on Edisto, but the land, the island. Her parents were planning to sell it—her father had had some financial reversals. But Verner Mackay saved it for her. He had plenty of money, thought it would be a nice place for hunting and picnics, that kind of thing. I don't think he ever considered living there full-time. He had his office downtown, a big house on Tradd Street.

Then my father retired. My parents needed more attention, and I was the only child. The building on King Street seemed a perfect location for a bookstore, and I'd learned a great deal about the book business from my uncle. My father—though he thought I'd lost my mind to turn my back on the tailoring business—let me have the space for next to nothing. I borrowed money for inventory, and the Book Nook was born.

I'd been back in Charleston a couple of years, just getting the business going, when she walked in. I had expected it would happen eventually—she was mad about books, devoured them, mostly history and biography—but I wasn't pre-pared for how I'd feel. She had Randall with her. He must have been nine or ten then. I remember being struck by—how shall I say it?—her coldness toward him, as if she felt inconvenienced by him. It was very strange. I took him by the hand and showed him the children's section, introduced him to the cats, and he played with them while we talked.

She told me she was spending most of her time on Edisto. "You must come for a visit sometime," she said, and I nodded, having no intention of ever doing so. I was still so hurt, and angry.

Over the next couple of years she'd stop by the store once or twice a month, sometimes with Randall, never with her husband. I'd seen a photo of Verner in the newspaper, but I'd never met him. Once or twice we had lunch together—she and I and the boy—and I began to feel more at ease around her. She wasn't flirtatious, really, but tremendously vivacious, a lively conversationalist. She al-ways made you feel that you were the most fascinating person she'd ever met. I'd been out with several women in New York, and a few after I returned to Charles-ton, but there was no real spark with any of them.

One day I received an invitation to Oak Bluff. "I'm having a small dinner party," she wrote. "Interesting people, no snobs. Who knows, you might meet someone!" Against my better judgment, I accepted.

She'd invited about ten people: a painter and her husband from Beaufort, the rest from Charleston and Edisto. There was a retired botanist, and a female playwright who wore earrings made of peacock feathers. One fellow—in the shrimping business, I think—knew even more about the island's history than Lila did. I found it odd that Lila's husband wasn't there, though she made some excuse about his being tied up with a business deal. We all drank too much—much more than I was accustomed to—and when the others left, she convinced me not to try the drive back to Charleston in the dark.

That was the beginning of the best and the worst year of my life. I'd go out there on Mondays—the bookshop was always closed on Mondays—spend the night, get up at the crack of dawn the next day to drive back to town. I lived for those times. The place—yes, you've seen it—was magical for me. I began to feel I belonged there. Lila's husband almost never came out, and the boy was still young enough that we imagined he didn't understand the nature of our relationship. She always referred to me as "our friend Simon." And indeed, I was his friend.

But one afternoon—he would have been about eleven or twelve, I would guess—Randall came home early from school. Lila had enrolled him in Porter-Gaud, and she paid someone to take him back and forth to Charleston. Anyway, that day, the school nurse had sent him home early because he felt ill. We didn't hear him come in the house. He caught us kissing. Of course, it could have been worse.

I shall never forget the look on that boy's face. "So, are you going to be my daddy now?" he asked. "Go to your room!" she shouted. I was horrified—none of this was his fault. When Randall left the room, I told her I wouldn't see her again unless she left Verner. For all intents and purposes, I argued, they were already separated. She promised she would, but of course she never did.

After that I would see her from time to time when she came into town, but always at the bookstore or in some public place, where there was no temptation. By that time Randall was in his early teens and he was beginning to get into trouble. Verner insisted that he move into Charleston, that he needed more discipline, and Lila—I sound very judgmental, but it's true—virtually abandoned him. Randall craved what neither of his parents gave him: their time, their attention, their love.

Lila and I remained friends until the end, though in her last years she rarely got into town anymore and I had stuck by my decision not to go back to Edisto, even after Verner passed away. I withheld my affection at a time when it might have meant a great deal to her. I did it out of pride, something that seems very petty now.

And I'm ashamed of this, but it was out of a need to punish her that I kept a secret from her. After his father died, Randall began to visit the bookstore again. I didn't recognize him. He was grown by then, but he would always gravitate toward the children's section—odd, of course, for a grown man. One day, one of my young employees whispered in my ear, "That one never buys. He just comes in to look at the kids' books and play with the cats." So I went up to him, asked if I could help him find anything. He mentioned a book, The Adventures of Mr. Pipweasel, *a children's storybook, English, lovely illustrations, but long out of print. I said I'd try to locate a copy. He wrote his name and address on a slip of paper and said, "You might remember me."*

He came back to the store many times before I sold it. I'd been told about his troubles with the law, his marital misadventures, but toward me he was always polite—he was strange, yes, but never antagonistic. I felt sorry for him. As I said, I remained in contact with Lila—mostly through our correspondence and the occasional phone call—but I never mentioned my friendship with Randall.

He seemed crushed when he learned I'd sold the bookstore, so I asked him if he'd like to come to one of my little Christmas gatherings—just my sister and my nephews and occasionally a neighbor or two. I didn't expect him to show up, but he came, brought a bottle of wine and some cookies. He's come every year since.

We never speak of Lila. It's the strangest thing, our connection. We have nothing in common except for our love for her, and our disappointment. And cats. He always loved cats.

I suppose you could say Randall is a lost soul—but then, aren't we all?

Heart Trouble

On the way home I stop at Harris Teeter for milk and eggs. "Never go grocery shopping when you're hungry," my mother has always said. By the time I make it to the checkout line my basket holds a tin of ginger cookies, a box of chocolate-covered cherries, an assortment of cheeses from the deli, a dozen tangerines, a precooked ham (for Mom and Delores), and a couple of white poinsettias in pots. Mom's always insisted that you can't have Christmas without poinsettias—"But not the red ones, they're so ordinary!"

When I get back to the condo parking garage and open my trunk I realize it's going to take me more than one trip to haul my purchases upstairs. "Damn!" I say out loud.

"That bad?" says a voice nearby. It's the doctor, the stethoscope draped around his neck. "I can help you with your groceries."

"Thanks, but I can—"

"You're the lawyer, right?" He lifts the poinsettias out of the trunk. "I'm on the floor below you. Next door to Mrs. Furley." The harsh light in the elevator accentuates the lines around his eyes, the shadows under them.

"Sally Baynard."

"Minh Basilier." He says his name slowly, as if to let me savor it: *Bah-SILL-ee-ay*. He sees me studying the name on the plastic ID card clipped to his white jacket. "I'm a New Orleans mongrel: Vietnamese and Cajun."

It seems rude not to invite him in. "Minh, this is my friend Delores. Delores, this is Minh Basilier." I'm pleased with myself for pronouncing it correctly.

"Nice to meet you," she says, turning down the volume on the TV.

"And this is Beatrice," I say, pointing to the cat, who's beside her on the sofa. "She's just here temporarily."

"Sure made herself right at home, though," says Delores. "Lucky for her I didn't do her in, just so I could get her magic bone!"

"What?"

She laughs. "It's a voodoo thing. If you carry the bone of a black cat, it gives you special powers. Like it can make you invisible, or help you bring back your lost lover."

"Where's Mom?" I ask.

"Back there with Mr. Shand and the dog, taking a nap."

"In the *bedroom*?"

"Old as they are, nothing much else going to happen."

I want to run back there, but now I have the doctor to deal with. "Would you like something to drink?" I ask him.

"Some other time," he says on his way out. "Looks like you've got your hands full."

When he's gone I turn to Delores. "I thought I made it clear—"

"Before you get all mad, go see for yourself. I'll put the groceries away."

The door to my mother's bedroom is open, the room dark except for the last of the daylight sifting through the curtains. Mom and Ed lie on their sides, fully clothed, his arm around her, his body spooning hers as if she were a child, her arm around Carmen, who hears my footsteps, looks up, then settles back on the pillow.

Delores's vegetable soup is warming on the stove, corn bread in the oven. I toss a salad, set two places at the kitchen table. Ed Shand won't get an invitation to dinner, and Delores has a date. I'm listening to NPR when Ed appears, amazingly unrumpled after his cuddle session. Ed is one of those never-a-stray-hair/always-good-posture men.

"That smells wonderful," he says, as if he lives here.

"We need to talk, Ed."

"It's not what you think."

"I'm not going to let you hurt her."

"*Hurt* her?"

"She's got Alzheimer's, Ed. She can't possibly understand your relationship, or whatever it is."

"I'm the best friend your mother has, except for Delores."

"Do you usually sleep with your best friends?"

"I haven't done anything . . . inappropriate," he says, turning red. "If you must know, I *can't* do anything. And of course I realize how ill she is. For some reason—maybe it's our . . . history together—I'm able to give her some comfort."

I'd like to slap him. "Your 'history' together?"

"We were both unhappy in our marriages."

"Did my father know about it?"

"I don't think so. He never said anything. But your father wasn't one to talk about his emotions."

"That doesn't mean he didn't have any."

"I know this is hard for you, but you must have known your parents' marriage wasn't a good one."

"My mother had unreasonable expectations."

"Is it unreasonable to expect a thoughtful Christmas present from your husband?" Ed asks.

"What are you talking about?"

"One year, shortly before your mother and I—before we fell in love—he gave her three handkerchiefs for Christmas. He'd picked them up at the dime store on his way home."

"Daddy didn't believe in expensive presents. We didn't have the money."

"But *handkerchiefs*? He didn't even bother to wrap them."

"So how long did the thing between you and Mom go on?"

"Two years, and then when he began to have the heart trouble, she ended it. But we remained friends."

"Maybe *you* gave him heart trouble."

He bristles. "That's not fair."

"It's not just a coincidence that you ended up here in Charleston, is it? In the very same building where my mother lives?"

"As a matter of fact, it *is* a coincidence. Before my wife died, we spent a lot of time in Charleston. She loved the restaurants, the Spoleto Festival, the architecture. She convinced me to buy the condo here, but right after we'd signed the contract she became ill, so she never got to enjoy it. It was sitting empty for a couple of years. I almost sold it, but my daughters were urging me to sell the big house in Columbia, so I decided to move. The change has been good for me. And finding your mother here was a miracle."

"I want you to stay away from her."

He retrieves his jacket from the hall closet, throws it over his shoulder. "Since you're such an expert on relationships, I'll let *you* explain to her why I've disappeared."

. . .

When Tony calls it's close to midnight, but I haven't slept. "Any news about the cat?" he asks.

"She's right here. It's a long story. I'll tell you all about it when you get back."

"So, what are you going to do with her?"

"I've almost made up my mind, but there are some logistics to work out. I'm leaning toward Gail, the caretaker, but she has a fiancé, and they don't want to move into Mrs. Mackay's house. Maybe I can change their minds. If not, does it really matter so much where the cat lives, as long as she's with someone who'll love her and take care of her? That's what matters to a cat, right?"

"That's what matters," he says. "To cats, to dogs. To everybody."

"But if Beatrice doesn't end up at Oak Bluff, I'll feel I've let her down."

"The cat?"

"Yes, but also Lila Mackay. I feel like . . . it's strange . . . like she's almost become a friend. Anyway, how's it going—with your son?"

"Better, I guess. We've been talking."

"Good."

"He might spend part of summer vacation with me. He can help out at the clinic—that way he won't be just sitting around the house."

"Good idea."

"I feel like I'm starting from scratch with him, almost."

"It's hard when you go for so long between visits."

"He won't say so, but I can tell he feels like I just dropped out of his life."

"You're not the one who moved to California," I say.

"But I haven't been trying hard enough. I have to make him my priority now."

There's a long silence, the only sound our breathing, then he says: "You weren't ever going to move in with me anyway, were you?"

"I'm trying to work it out, Tony."

"You've been saying that for quite a while."

"Didn't you just say you have to make your son the priority now?"

"I didn't mean it *that* way."

"Let's talk about it later. I hate the telephone."

"How's the beagle?" he asks.

"She's sleeping with Mom. Seems right at home. She's got this raw place on her leg, though. She keeps gnawing it."

"Does it look infected?" he asks.

"No, it's just kind of . . . a place where she's rubbed the hair off."

"It's probably stress. She's getting accustomed to her new surroundings."

"She seemed really upset when the cat was missing. Like she knew something was wrong. Sometimes I think we don't give animals enough credit. But she's better now."

"Okay, I'll let you get back to sleep," he says. "Take care."

"You, too."

After we hang up it feels like the silence is full of things unsaid, and it's only the cat's steady purring that eases me back into sleep.

For Old Times' Sake

———◆———

I'd looked forward to the drive out to Edisto, a morning away from the office. Maybe, I hoped, the cat would do me a favor and ride quietly, distracted by her fake mouse. But Delores called in sick, so now I have my mother in the backseat, with the howling cat, and Carmen in the front with me. Carmen's amazingly calm, resigned to the cat's moods. Or maybe she's just exhausted from the commotion of the past few days. She closes her eyes, rests her chin on her paws. I wish I had her attitude.

"We need to go back to the condo!" shouts my mother.

"But you *like* plantations!" I shout back.

"We forgot Ed!"

"Ed can't come today, Mom."

In the rearview mirror I watch her face crumple, and then, as we pass Rutledge Avenue, the tears rolling down her cheeks, little rivulets through the makeup she applied by herself, too heavily. I'm thinking I'd better turn around, go back home, call Shenille to see if she can stay with Mom. And then I see him: the old man in the black hat and overcoat, walking with a cane up Gadsden Street. It's Simon Witowski. The wind's blowing hard against him, and just as I pass

Gadsden, it lifts his hat and tosses it into the air. He turns to search for it, and something about this—the old man by himself, the hat sailing down the street—convinces me to turn the car around.

"Oh, hello!" he says when I pull up next to him.

"I think it blew into those bushes," I say, pointing.

"Is that Ed?" asks my mother.

"No, Mom."

We never find the hat. He was just out taking his morning walk, he says. He tries to get out every day unless it's raining. But it's colder than he realized, so yes, it would be nice to take a little ride; it's been a long time since he visited Oak Bluff. Yes, that would be nice. For old times' sake.

And that's how Simon Witowski ends up in the backseat with my mother, the cat in her carrier between them, quieter now. "She's a gorgeous creature, isn't she?" he says.

"Thank you!" my mother answers, though he wasn't talking about her.

"Lila refused to pave this road," Simon says as we bump along the dirt road to the house. "She always said she wanted people to slow down, so they would notice the world around them. Look—that's a big one, isn't he?" The buck's antlers catch the sunlight before he darts into the brush.

"We can't stay long," I explain. "Gail's just meeting me here so that she can lead me to her trailer—we're going to meet her boyfriend there." But I know my mother will enjoy seeing the house, and Simon has already assumed the role of tour guide.

"Oak Bluff was constructed about 1800," he says. "By then Lila's great-great-grandfather, who built it, had gotten rich off sea island cotton, a variety that was only grown on the islands of South Carolina, Georgia, and northern Florida." I stop the car, and before I know it, Simon's helping my mother out, a maneuver he somehow accomplishes while leaning on his cane. "There's a story that the Pope's garments were made from Edisto Island cotton. "

"The Pope was here?" asks my mother.

"No, but the Marquis de Lafayette was entertained at a plantation just down the road," says Simon. "Of course, the wealth would not have been possible without slavery. All the planting and the picking was done by hand. It was backbreaking labor." He looks down toward the river. "Lila loved this place, and she could be sentimental, but she was also an expert on its history. I think it haunted her."

Beatrice knows she's home. With a shrill "meow" she demands to be let out of the carrier. "Not yet," I say, lifting it. "Wait till we get inside." Carmen's already bounded out of the car, and we wait while she relieves herself behind a camellia bush. "Okay, honey," I say to her, "if you behave yourself, you can come in, too."

There's a fire in the fireplace on the ground floor, a stack of wood at the end of the hearth, and Lila's old quarters have been swept and dusted, the books removed from the long table behind the sofa and put back on the bookshelves, the papers organized in neat stacks on the desk. "Ah," says Simon, "she loved this room in winter. So much cozier than the ones upstairs." There's something simmering in a pot on the stove, but Gail's not in the kitchen. I settle Simon and Mom on the sofa in front of the fire, the cat in Simon's care.

The beagle follows me up the stairs. Gail's in the dining room, sorting through the papers on the long table. "Oh, I didn't hear you come in," she says, and when she turns toward me I see the purple bruise around her eye, the red mark across her cheek.

"What happened?"

She touches her face. "Billy."

The story she tells is a variation of the one I've heard in my office a hundred times: *This isn't the first time, but it's the worst. I've finally made up my mind.* She hopes it's okay that she's been staying here for a few days. "He was lying to me the whole time," she says. "He has a wife and two kids in North Charleston. The trailer belongs to *her.* I guess *she* had enough sense to get away, too."

"I'm sorry," I say. "You should get a restraining order."

"He won't bother me anymore," she says. "Not after what I did to him." He'd chased her around the trailer, pushed her against the re-frigerator, "but I grabbed a saucepan off the stove. It wasn't hot or anything, but I hit him pretty hard. For a minute I thought I'd killed him . . . and you know what? I wasn't even sorry. It was like . . . when he came to, he had this whole different look on his face, like he finally understood he wasn't going to mess with me anymore. And you know what else? Since I been here, it's almost like she . . . It's hard to explain, but I feel like Lila's here with me, that's she's proud of me. . . . Where's Beatrice?"

"Downstairs. I brought my mother, and an old friend of Lila's. I hope that's okay."

"Sure."

"The house looks great, by the way. You've been doing a lot of work."

"I just thought, as long as I was here I might as well. . . . And I was thinking that when the weather warms up a little I can start painting the outside. But if you've found someone else, I can be out tomorrow." She touches the bruise again. "My sister lives up in Sum-merville; she has an extra bedroom."

"Before I drove out here I felt you were the best choice, but I was concerned that you didn't want to live here. But if you've changed your mind, that's ideal. It's what Lila wanted—for Beatrice to live here."

"So I can stay?"

"As long as you're willing to take on the responsibility."

"I feel like . . . like it's kind of an honor. To be chosen."

"What about your other cats?" I remember what Tony said about cats being territorial.

"Billy wouldn't let me take them. He's nicer to them than he is to me."

"So, you feel okay about staying here alone? What about the ghost?"

"It's funny, since I been here—since I got away from Billy—I'm not afraid of anything anymore. And I won't be alone. I'll have Beatrice."

"Come downstairs and meet Lila's old friend, Simon Witowski." But I hear Simon and my mother across the hall, in the living room, and Beatrice, loosed from her carrier, has found Gail.

"Good heavens!" Mom says, peering into the living room. "This place could certainly use a decorator!" She's breathless from the climb.

Simon's at one of the big windows. "Look, Margaret," he says, his arm on her elbow again, "from here you can see the river, and beyond that . . . see? . . . the ocean."

But Mom is busy surveying the room. "It could be a showplace, but it would take a lot of work," she says. "And even if we could afford it, the problem is finding good help. These days it's almost impossible to find good help. So I think it might be too much for us, don't you?"

Simon's response is perfect: "You're right, Margaret. It would be too much. But we can enjoy the visit, can't we?"

"And besides," she says, "my daughter says there's a ghost."

"There's a ghost, all right," says Simon. "But he's a friendly one.

He was in love here, and though it turned out badly for him, he keeps coming back—looking for her, hoping she'll change her mind. *I'm* the ghost."

"But you're not dead!" she says.

"It's the ghost of my younger self," he says. "He's a dreamer. He just won't give up."

Watching the Tide Go Out

—————◦∘◦—————

We *should have a Christmas party,* said Mom, and I said *Maybe,* hoping she'd forget, but these days her brain's a grab bag: She'll reach in and pull out a surprise, often a story from decades ago, less often something that happened recently, and more and more, something that hasn't happened at all. She'll insist that someone has stolen her diamond necklace, though she's never had a diamond necklace, or she'll tell me she needs to take her Cadillac in for repairs, though it was Ed Shand's wife who had the Cadillac.

But she didn't forget my *Maybe,* and somehow it morphed into this gathering, the first party I've had since I moved to the condo. The guest list started small—Delores, Shenille, Ellen and Hank, Gina, Tony, Gail Sims, and Simon Witowski—but then took on a life of its own.

Delores is here with her friend from the choir, a tall, balding baritone with a nice smile. Shenille brings her sister, makes up some excuse about why her husband can't come. My old law school friends, Wendy and Valerie, are here, too, with their husbands, because Ellen said, *If it gets back to them that you had a party, they'll be really pissed.*

But it isn't really a party, I'd said, *just a few people, because my mother won't let it go.*

As long as you're doing it, she'd continued, *you might as well do it right. What's the difference if you have to wash a few more plates and glasses? And why don't you get someone to cater it so you can enjoy yourself? What about that guy at Harris Teeter, your old client? He'd love to do it.*

Gina and Mandy arrive together. I hadn't included Mandy on the original list because I wanted Ellen to have a night off from worrying about her, but Gina had said, *She's just moved in. I'd feel bad about leaving her alone right now.* So here's my secretary getting a drink for Mandy, declining Donnie's offer of champagne: "She's pregnant. Do you have some ginger ale?"

When I'd called Gail, she asked if she could bring Simon. *He sent me the nicest letter, telling me how happy Lila would have been that Beatrice is in good hands,* she said. *He's not too happy about moving into that retirement place. I was thinking maybe he could spend a weekend out here every now and then. I come into Charleston sometimes, you know, and I could pick him up. I'd like the company, and Beatrice . . . Beatrice adores him. And maybe he could keep some of his books here. He doesn't have room for them where he's going. If it's okay with you.*

Sure, I'd said. *That would be nice. And Gail, you don't need my permission to have guests. You're in charge now.*

I'll bring Beatrice, too—to the party, I mean. I don't like to leave her by herself for too long.

Mrs. Furley is here, without Curley, the poodle. "Oh, I didn't know this was a pet-friendly party," she says when she sees the beagle and the cat. Right behind her is Minh Basilier, minus his stethoscope. I make the mistake of introducing him as Dr. Basilier, and immediately Mrs. Furley is consulting him about her arthritis.

There are absences. Joe Baynard sent his regrets, though I hadn't intended to invite him. Mom saw him at church and blurted out that we were having a party, so I had no choice. *It was nice of you to include us,* he e-mailed, *but Susan and I are taking the boys skiing over Christmas.* He's disappointed that I haven't agreed to help him with his campaign for the circuit judgeship.

Tony calls in the middle of the party, says he's sorry, he's had a tough day at the clinic, he's exhausted. "I understand," I say. I'll call him tomorrow, suggest we meet for dinner. I've known for a while now what I need to say, though I'm not quite sure how. I only know it's not the kind of thing you should say over the telephone.

For a while I'm worried that Ed Shand won't show—I've promised Mom he's coming—but here he is, with a bottle of wine and a present for her, beautifully wrapped. It was Delores who made me reconsider. *You think real hard before you break her heart—you hear me? Her mind's a mess, but she's still got her heart.*

Ann Wilson, the new probate judge, signed the Final Order in the Mackay case this afternoon. I have a certified copy for Gail, and I'll send another one to Randall Mackay, with a letter:

Dear Mr. Mackay:

I've completed my duties as enforcer of your mother's trust. I'm enclosing a certified copy of Judge Wilson's Order. You will see that I've chosen Gail Sims as caregiver for Beatrice. As you know, under the terms of the trust, the cat's caregiver will reside at Oak Bluff so long as Beatrice is alive.

As I'm sure you will understand, my role as trust enforcer has been to fulfill your mother's wishes as set forth in the trust, not to substitute my judgment for hers.

I want to remind you that upon Beatrice's death, you will have possession of Oak Bluff, provided, of course, that you do nothing to harm the cat. Your friend Simon Witowski, who knows you far better than I do, assures me this warning is unnecessary, but I can't conclude my work on this case without reiterating it.

I am enclosing a little book your mother kept, which I think may interest you. This "diary" was included in the box of things she left relating to the trust. At first I had difficulty understanding it, because it is told from Beatrice's point of view. I can only guess why your mother did that. Perhaps she was merely trying to imagine what it's like to see the world through another creature's eyes. Perhaps she had difficulty expressing her feelings, and it was easier to write from behind a mask. If you look at the page I've marked, you'll see some evidence for this latter theory.

Sincerely,

Sarah Bright Baynard

This is the paragraph I've marked, written in Lila's shaky hand:

I'm sitting beside her on the dock, at sundown, watching the tide go out. "When I was a girl," she says, "I thought life was like the tides, the water going out but always coming back in, the losses always replenished. I was mistaken."

I'm a lucky cat. She loves me with all her heart, but when she takes me in her arms, as she does this evening, I feel, in a strange way, that I've profited from her mistakes, that I'm the beneficiary of her regrets.

But enough of that—it's almost dark, and time for dinner! She'll tell me I'm too fat, then fill my bowl to the brim.